Playing By His Rules

Glenda Horsfall

www.blackvelvetseductions.com

ISBN 978-1-936556-62-5

All characters in this book are completely fictional. They exist only in the imagination of the author. Any similarity to any actual person or persons, living or dead, is completely coincidental.

Published 2015
Printed by Black Velvet Seductions Publishing
A division of Savage Publications

Visit us at:
www.blackvelvetseductions.com

www.blackvelvetseductions.com

Chapter One

Shit. Shit. Shit! Xander couldn't believe it. It was bad enough that the papers had published the story, but for it to come out now, when he was visiting his sister, was worse than bad luck. Sophia was going to kill him for bringing bedlam to her home.

He paced his brother-in-laws study like a caged animal. His cell phone had started ringing in the early hours of the morning; the newshounds were out for blood. He knew it wouldn't be long before they tracked him to Sophia's home. He wasn't concerned for himself, Christ he couldn't give a damn what they thought about him, but he needed to make plans to get away from his sister's home before the paparazzi realized he was here and started camping on his sister's doorstep. Getting away from here would ensure that the paparazzi now hounding him did not inadvertently get photographs of his niece and nephews. Therefore, he needed to remove himself from the vicinity of the family home as soon as possible. Sophia would never forgive him if his actions brought unwanted attention to her family. There had been numerous high profile kidnappings in Greece, and they had made the decision not to allow photographs of the children to appear in the press.

Deep in thought, he was less than cordial when his cell phone rang yet again. A quick glance at the display ascertained it was Giles, his security chief, based in Athens.

"What now?" He snapped, his tone harsh.

"We have a situation here–"

"Well, handle it. That's what I pay you for!" Shit! He couldn't hide out here and have his sister's life disrupted.

"Look Giles, you'll have to excuse me, it's been quite a night and I've had no sleep." He continued in a more even tone, "Whatever is going on down there, just sort it. You have carte blanche to take whatever action you deem necessary."

"Very well, Mr. Doumas," Giles came back sounding his normal controlled self, "I'll order extra security for the house and have Mrs. Stephanos transferred to her sister's."

Damn, it looked like he wasn't going to return to his Athens home either. According to Giles, the press were already camped on the doorstep there and his elderly housekeeper had been forced to lock herself inside the house. What a bloody mess!

"I have a few things to tie up here before I leave," Xander returned, "but I want you to send the helicopter to Santorini to pick me up at noon. Have the jet on standby at the airport. I'll let you know later where we're headed so that the pilot can file a flight plan."

"Very well, Sir."

Feeling relieved now that he had arranged to remove himself from Santorini, he sat down heavily in the large leather chair behind the desk. Once again, he cast his eyes over the computer screen where he had pulled up copies of the newspaper articles published that morning. Just the sight of the newspaper headlines was enough to have his temper spiking. "Billionaire with Perverted Tastes" and "CEO with Kinky Sex Life" were two of the milder ones. The accompanying pictures which showed the inside of his private play room along with a photo of his ex-girlfriend, nude and tied to the St Andrews Cross, had him cursing as he thumped the desk in frustration. He hoped the thump he had inflicted on the table had not woken the household. Nursing his aching knuckles, which would surely show bruises within a few hours, he cursed Marie under his breath. The bitch would not get away with this. He would make her pay for the havoc she had brought down upon his head. He had no doubt that Marie herself had provided the pictures because she had threatened to go to the media.

He wished now he had taken her blackmail attempt more seriously. He really hadn't believed she would have the nerve to go through with a 'kiss and tell all' story. Now look at the bloody mess he was in. What was worse was that gut instinct told him it was going to get worse before it got better.

Outside, all still appeared quiet, but he had taken the additional precaution of calling in extra security to patrol the perimeter of his sister's property. Dawn would be breaking soon, and tired as he was, he still had a lot to do before noon, when the helicopter would be arriving to pick him up.

He spent the next hour on the phone putting his plans into action. He didn't think twice about getting his lawyer out of bed in the middle of the night, giving him terse instructions with regard to the newspaper editors and his ex-girlfriend. They would all be sorry that they had crossed him. By the time he finished with them they would wish they had never heard his name.

He looked up as the study door opened and Georgiou entered carrying a couple of large coffee mugs.

"I heard you up and about. Problems?" He crossed the room to place a welcome cup of coffee on the desk in front of him.

"Sorry I disturbed you. Is Sophia–"

"Sophia is still asleep," Georgiou cut in, "and by the look of you I would say that's a good thing. You look like hell. What's going on?"

"That!" He pointed towards the computer screen, before twisting it around in order that Georgiou could read it from the opposite side of the desk. He watched the emotions flicker across his brother-in-law's face.

Xander remained silent as his brother-in-law read the articles, occasionally stopping to glance across at him. He did not have to say anything, the looks he threw Xander's way spoke volumes. His eyes widened and his eyebrows rose as he glanced between him and the computer screen, as though he could not believe what he was reading. His face occasionally broke into a spontaneous grin as he cast Xander a quick sideways glance. It was obvious to Xander that his brother-in-law found his predicament amusing.

"Well, well. I never would have believed it, you always seemed so straightforward." Georgiou grinned, before he continued, "Never would have had you down for one to play kinky games." He held up his hands in an open gesture. "Not that it bothers me. What you do behind closed doors is your own business. However, I don't think your sister is going to be too amused when she sees the papers."

Looking over at him, Xander grimaced as he raked his fingers back through his hair, "Tell me about it, that's one conversation I'm not looking forward to. She's going to give me hell!"

'Hell' was an understatement. When Sophia finally tracked him down in the study, she looked like she wanted to commit murder. He was, most definitely, not her favorite person at the moment. That shook Xander to his core. Her look of disappointment made his stomach churn, and he held himself rigid as he struggled not to turn away from her. The guilt he felt at disappointing her gnawed away at his insides until he felt sick. He was used to Sophia looking at him with something akin to hero worship. The look of disdain on her face hurt far more than he could have imagined. He held his breath and braced for her attack.

"What have I told you in the past about the types of girlfriends you choose?" Christ, she sounded more like his mother than his younger sister, not surprising really, as she had tried to mother him ever since they had lost their parents in an accident when she was just seventeen. Xander had been twenty-one at the time and had become the head of their small family, taking guardianship of his sister and raising her as his parents would have wished. Sophia had clung to him at first, but over time had settled into running their small household, keeping the home they shared comfortable and trying to fill her mother's role.

At that moment, he was grateful his mother wasn't around to witness his fall from grace. He could only imagine what she would have had to say. It was bad enough that Sophie was here to witness the media coverage of his sex life. Christ, could there be anything worse than having your sex life laid out for public discussion? Was nothing sacred any more?

His thoughts were all over the place and he battled to keep his emotions in check. He was angry with Marie for discussing their private life. Hell, there was nothing wrong with his sex life, he knew that. He was not a sadist or into pain, he enjoyed giving women pleasure. He knew however that many people didn't understand the BDSM lifestyle and mistook it for abuse. He was irritated and embarrassed to be put in the position of having to explain his lifestyle to his sister of all people.

Hardly pausing for breath she continued, her voice rising with every word until she was shouting at him. "Why can't you find a decent girl and settle down, instead of cavorting with bimbos?" Her tone betrayed her disgust at the types of women he dated as much as the newspaper headlines.

"What's wrong with you?" She continued to rant, "Why can't you date a nice Greek girl, a girl from a good family? One who would look after you?" She turned away from him as she paced the study.

"They'd bore me to death." He responded automatically, without giving himself time to consider his answer or her reaction.

She spun on her heel, glaring at him and he wished he'd kept his mouth shut. "Hah! And you're telling me the air heads you date don't?"

She shook her head, obviously deeply saddened by his plight. Crossing the room, she reached towards him, and grasped his hands. Softly, she asked, "What's wrong with dating a decent girl, one who will make a good wife? You need a proper girlfriend, someone who can converse intelligently and help you at business functions. You need someone who will be happy to have a family and make a home for you."

"I don't date them for their conversation," he responded dryly, exasperated. The last thing he needed was Sophia feeling sorry for him, "And I can handle my business perfectly well without saddling myself with a wife."

"Why bother dating them if you have no intention of taking the relationship any further?"

Surely, she wasn't that naïve? He said nothing only raised his brow in reply as he looked at her. He knew she had understood his silent answer when he saw the tell tale flush of embarrassment on her face.

Looking more distressed by the minute, she choked, "You should be ashamed of yourself, having a room like that built in your home. I am never going to live this down! How am I going to face my friends after this?"

She was clearly upset, her cheeks glowed and he was, for once in his life, at a loss for words. He did not want to discuss his lifestyle with his sister, nor did he want her to have to explain his behavior to her friends. He struggled to keep his temper in check; irritated at the predicament Marie had caused. It would be better for Sophia if he took himself out of circulation for a while. Maybe the old saying 'out of sight, out of mind' would be true. If the media couldn't track him down the story would die a natural death.

"So, what are you going to do?" She glared at him from across the room. "Have you seen the circus outside? The paparazzi are gathering at the gates. They are like vultures. Two helicopters have already flown low over the gardens. I've had to order all the drapes kept closed and confine the children to the nursery for the day!"

Shit! The newshounds hadn't taken as long as he'd thought they would to find out his whereabouts. He had really hoped that he would have left Santorini before they realized he was visiting with Sophia.

"I'm sorry, Sophia," he whispered, his voice full of remorse. All his life he had done everything he could to protect his younger sister. Christ, it was just his luck that the story had broken while he was here.

"Sorry is not going to fix this!"

"Listen to me, Sophia," he said, his voice now firm. "I've made arrangements to leave. I'll be out of your hair within the next couple of hours. As soon as they see me leave the paparazzi will disperse and leave you in peace." He raked his fingers through his hair. "The bastards will be too busy chasing me to bother you."

For the first time she looked sympathetic. "Where are you going to go?"

"Scotland. The house there is remote and the press is a lot less intrusive there than they are on the Continent. The story will be a ten day wonder, it will all be forgotten about in a few weeks."

"But it's so isolated!" She cried. Grasping his hands tight, and with tears in her eyes, she pleaded with him to reconsider. "What the hell are you going to do there on your own? It's not going to be much fun!" She shook her head. "Stay here with us. The paps will soon get sick of hanging around."

Xander sighed, "Don't be silly Sophia, I can't stay here now. That lot," he said through gritted teeth, as he pointed towards the window behind the closed drapes, "will never give you peace while I am here. There is no way I'm taking any chances with the children."

"But who will look after you?"

He couldn't help but laugh, "I'm a big boy, Sophia, and I am perfectly capable of taking care of myself. I have already advertised for help." He pulled her close to hug her tight, and felt guilty all over again when he felt her tremble. He bent and kissed her gently on her forehead, "I'll be fine Sophia, stop worrying. A few weeks on the island will give me a break. You keep telling me I should have a holiday."

She pulled away from him and hugged herself as she rocked back and forward on her feet. He cursed Marie for causing his sister distress. "I know I told you to take a break, but I was thinking more a month here at home relaxing, sailing, sun bathing. I sure as hell wasn't thinking about you going to Scotland in March on your own. It will be cold and miserable!"

"It will be a peaceful and refreshing. All that sea air will be invigorating," he assured her. In truth, he relished the prospect of a few weeks of isolated peace and quiet. He enjoyed his downtime on the island as it was one of the few places where he could have total privacy.

***

Xander shook his head in dismay. Leaving Santorini and shaking the paparazzi off his tail had been the easy bit. Getting staff to join him in his isolation was proving harder than he had thought. The advert had been running for ten days nationwide and he was surprised at how few applications he had received. Looking at the cover letters with résumés attached he was dismayed at his lack of choice. He could have flown in a secretary or bookkeeper from any of his offices around the world but, thinking about the high end corporate offices in some of the most vibrant cities in the world, he didn't think any of them would take too kindly to working on an isolated island for more than a brief time. He was also absolutely positive that they wouldn't be prepared to do housework or cooking. He wanted someone who would be content and who was happy to entertain themselves; after all, the island was no metropolis and there was certainly no night life.

Reading through the applications again it looked like his choice was down to one of three applicants, all of which looked suitable on paper and had the necessary qualifications to do what he required. As the applicants all lived in different areas of the country he decided on a central location and fired off replies to all three stating that he would arrange overnight accommodation and cover travelling expenses. Interviews were set for three days hence and he prepared himself for a trip to London.

He opted to stay at his apartment above the London office at Canary Wharf as he could take the helicopter from the airport, land on the roof, and enter the building unseen. Even though the media frenzy had died down, he still didn't want the attention. He would be in and out of town before the press even knew he had left the island.

Chapter Two

'Craftsman requires Housekeeper/Girl Friday. Must be efficient, able to work without supervision. Computer literate helpful. Irregular working hours occasionally required but plenty of down time. Live-In position due to rural location. Good remuneration package for the right candidate. Immediate start required. Must be free to travel. Apply by email to Xander@islandcrafts.com'

Chloe had been trawling the net for days looking for a suitable position and had almost given up when the advert, in bold print, jumped out at her. It looked like the answer to all her prayers, an income and accommodation. She would be able to leave town quickly and have the means to relocate.

Nick, her shit of an ex-boyfriend, was due to be released from prison in just twenty-one days, after serving six months jail time for his assault on her. At the time he'd been sentenced she'd estimated three months would give her plenty of time to recover her strength and vanish before his release, but she had taken longer to heal than anticipated and now she was starting to panic that he would be free before she could make her escape. She had to move soon; staying where she was, was no longer an option and unless she secured a job soon she would have no funds to relocate and would be trapped. The position advertised promised funds and a roof over her head, with the added bonus of being far away from Nick.

The very thought of having to face him again made her feel sick. With trembling fingers she swiftly typed a response to the advert and fired off her résumé to the unknown Xander. Chloe only hoped that when he said 'immediate start' he meant now!

Three days later, she received the reply she had been anxiously awaiting. She had been invited to attend an interview at a well-known upmarket London hotel. She was to present herself at reception at the given time and would be met by a member of staff and escorted to the interview suite. Her excitement blended with the first hope she'd felt in a long time and blossomed in her chest. She was determined to make a good impression and secure the position she so desperately needed.

Xander entered the hotel lounge and sat down at the bar. It was nearly midnight and the area was reasonably quiet. At least he didn't expect to bump into any newshounds at this time of night, and especially not here. It wasn't the kind of place the rich and famous frequented, more a local hotel.

After ordering his usual, Jack Daniels on the rocks, he casually looked around surveying the other occupants. There were several men in a booth in the corner. It was obvious from their dress and snippets of their conversation that they were City bankers. The empty champagne bottles on their table hinted at some sort of celebration. There were a few couples at tables around the lounge. He expected they were finishing off their night with a drink before retiring.

Tucked away in the corner by herself, he spotted a blond. Her long hair shielded her face as she sat head down, book in one hand drink in the other. She seemed oblivious to the raucous conversation going on in the booth next to her as the bankers backslapped and congratulated each other on the deal they had closed. He was intrigued. It was unusual to see a lone woman in a hotel lounge this late in the evening. Well, unusual if they weren't hookers.

He watched her for a while expecting a partner or friend to join her, but it became obvious that she was alone. Something about her stillness appealed to him and he continued to watch her as he sipped his drink. She seemed to be an oasis of calm in the middle of a storm. His curiosity about her grew and he wished she would lift her head so he could see her face.

A loud crash reverberated around the room as one of the bankers knocked an empty champagne bottle off the table. The woman jumped and dropped her book. The drink she had been holding sloshed and spilled across her lap. Her head snapped around turning towards the sound. For the first time he was able to get a look at her face. He caught his breath at her exquisite features. The long wavy blond hair framed a heart shaped face with high cheekbones. Her delicate shaped brows the perfect outline for her vivid blue eyes, which reminded him of the blue sky of Santorini in summer. She had a perfect Cupid's bow of a mouth and he found himself imagining how she would taste. Would she taste cool and refreshing, a balm to his troubled spirit, or would she burn like the Mediterranean sun?

From across the room, he could see her visibly relax when she realized the crash was caused by no more than a careless accident. She continued to scan the room as if checking that there were no other threats present. Seeming satisfied, she bent to pick up the book she had dropped. Looking at the wet table, she shook her head, before turning to place the book on the chair at her side. Lifting her purse, she rummaged through the contents with one hand while she shook the other.

Grabbing a towel from the bar, he walked across the room to introduce himself and help her clean up. Raising her head, as though she had sensed him, her clear blue eyes met his as he advanced. She quickly glanced around as if to see where he was heading. He watched as she nibbled at her lip and a small frown furrowed her brow. His imagination went into overdrive at the thought of what her mouth could do to him. As he continued his approach, time seemed to slow. Although she now met his eyes, her look was wary and she held herself completely still. Her posture immediately brought to mind a small doe he had spotted in the forest around his home. He had come across the doe accidently and she had frozen on the spot, sniffing the air around her, before turning and running in the opposite direction. If he didn't know better he would say the woman was preparing to take flight and he wondered what or who had made her so edgy. He raised an eyebrow in query, wordlessly requesting permission to come closer, and she blushed delicately in response.

The light flush betrayed her vulnerability and brought out his need to protect. Up close, he was even more enamored. He stopped at her table, handing her the towel to blot up the drink she had spilled as he stood looking down at her. At her shy smile of thanks he murmured, "I thought you could do with some help."

"Thanks, again." Her voice was soft and low, and he once again felt desire unfurl low in his stomach.

"As we're apparently the only two singles in the bar do you mind if I join you?"

Her gaze once again flicked to the hotel security at the door. He was glad that she was being cautious. He extended his hand, "I'm harmless," he assured her.

With a little nod in his direction, she extended her hand towards him. Her handshake was firm, but he was aware of the feel of her satin soft skin, before she gently pulled her hand free and indicated the free stool at the opposite side of the table. She was a shy little thing, obviously unaware of her own appeal. She nibbled on her bottom lip, an action he found incredibly erotic. Shit, he really had been too long without a woman if such a small thing could turn him on.

Straddling the stool, he was caught unaware when he tried to introduce himself. "I'm--"

"No names. We're strangers meeting in a bar." She held up her hands to forestall him. The tip of her tongue slipped out to delicately moisten her lips. "You don't need to know my name."

"What?" What the hell did that mean? What was she hiding? "I have to call you something--"

"'Something' will do." She giggled.

"Now, you're being silly," he teased, as he wondered how much of a night cap she had actually had.

"No, I'm not." For the first time she looked directly at him, and he caught a flash of irritation in her eyes. She hadn't appreciated being called silly, and he cursed himself for being an idiot. She obviously had her reasons for making her request, and he had just belittled them. She continued, with a hint of determination, "I like my privacy and a girl has to think about her safety nowadays." She closed her eyes briefly, as if in pain. "I'm quite happy to have a drink and a chat, but that's as far as it goes. You don't need to know my name for that."

Surprise shot through him. If the bar hadn't been so quiet, he would have thought he had misheard her. In his normal circle, women clamored to know everything they could about him. They sure as hell made sure he knew exactly who they were and how he could find them again. His wealth seemed to draw them like a magnet. Even though he had intended nothing more than a half hour or so of convivial company, he wasn't used to being dismissed so casually. He wanted her to want to know more about him.

"Well then, Angel," there was no way he was going to call her 'something' and the endearment just tripped off his tongue, "can I get you a refill?" He asked, indicating her now near empty glass.

Chloe picked up her glass and drained the remaining contents slowly, as she surveyed him over the rim.

"Yes, please." She handed over the now empty vessel, "Another dark rum and cola would be great. No ice."

"Back shortly." She watched as he strode towards the bar to place their order. He briefly acknowledged others in the bar as he passed them, but did not stop to chat. Even from the rear, he was an attractive man. Now that he was not watching her, she allowed herself a moment to admire him. His broad shoulders tapered to a neat waist. He had long muscular legs and a tight butt, all of which were encased in black denim. She found herself wondering what he did for a living. Was it something physical which kept him in such good shape or did he work out to maintain his sculpted physique?

Delicious tingles vibrated through her as she recalled the sound of his voice. He spoke perfect English but with a slight accent and she surmised he was European, possibly Italian or Greek, judging by his coloring. He had a light tan and raven black hair, which he wore slightly longer than collar length. She gave herself a mental pat on the back, feeling very pleased with herself for being able to attract the interest of such a gorgeous man. He had taken her request for 'no names' in his stride apparently and he seemed to still want her company.

Things were looking up. For so long she had felt unattractive and had deliberately dressed down to appease Nick. Now it was time for her to please herself, to do what she wanted to do, to go where she wanted to go. No longer would she take orders from a control freak.

If her interview in the morning went well, she would be on her way to creating a new life for herself. A life free of restriction and fear. For tonight, she was going to allow herself a little light flirtation.

He had his back turned towards her as he ordered their drinks at the bar. She found herself watching his interaction with the barman. From her seat, she couldn't hear what they were discussing but, from the sound of the laughter she caught, she surmised they were exchanging jokes.

He turned suddenly to glance in her direction, breaking into a large grin when he caught her eye. Mortified to be caught staring, she glanced away quickly, but not before she saw the wink he threw in her direction. *Confident bastard.* He was looking very pleased with himself whereas she was feeling flustered. Butterflies flitted around in her stomach and she took a deep breath. It had been so long since she had felt this pull of attraction, so long since she had even dared to look at a man other than Nick. The last time she had glanced at a man, well, a waiter to be honest, Nick had broken her arm. She shuddered at the memory.

She reminded herself that she had an interview to attend in the morning. If she got the post, and she desperately hoped she was successful, then she wasn't going to be around to see tall, dark and gorgeous again. She couldn't afford to get involved with anyone.

She was glad now that she hadn't divulged her name. Even if he wanted to see her again, he wouldn't be able to find her. The idea was kind of liberating. Tonight she could be anyone or anything she wanted. She could allow herself to enjoy her time with him and leave when it was over with no strings.

Watching as he returned, she couldn't help but notice other women following him with their eyes. It wasn't only because he looked good, it was his designer clothes, his discreet gold jewelry, it was the confident way he carried himself. All of which marked him as a wealthy man. His long legged stride soon ate up the distance between them. He gave no indication that he saw the admiring glances of the women in the room. He kept his eyes firmly fixed on her and the butterflies in her stomach took flight at the gleam in his eyes.

When he reached the table, he handed over her drink and placed a large bowl of fat olives on the table between them.

"Help yourself." He indicated the dish, before straddling the stool opposite her. He appeared totally relaxed and at ease with himself as he snagged a plump olive, biting it in half between his even white teeth, before popping the second half into his mouth. He chewed slowly as though savoring the taste, and her eyes were drawn to his lips, now lightly coated with olive oil. They looked full and inviting and she wondered how it would feel to have those lips upon her own. Would he be the type to offer soft teasing kisses, which seduced her into surrender? On the other hand, would he be demanding, the take control, sure of himself, alpha male?

Raising her eyes, she felt her stomach flip as she saw him looking at her as though he had read her thoughts. Nervous tension raced through her as they regarded each other silently. In the end, she was unable to hold his gaze. He was just too overwhelming and she rushed into conversation to break the silence.

"So, umm… Are you in town on business or do you live locally?" She asked.

He smiled widely, as if he was aware he had knocked her equilibrium off balance. "I travel a lot," he told her, "but my main home is in Athens." This didn't really answer her question. *Main home. How many homes did he have?*

"So, you are here on business?"

"No. Not this time." The smile slipped from his face, and for just a second he appeared grim. "I am taking a little time out. Having a short break." His voice was clipped, making her think there was something about the break he found unpleasant.

"And you choose to holiday in Britain? In March?" she asked in disbelief. Why the hell would someone with a home in the sun, and obviously the means to go anywhere he wanted, choose to visit London where the weather was miserable at this time of year?

He shrugged his shoulders. "A change is as good as a rest, or so they tell me." His chocolate brown eyes were alight with humor, as if her questions amused him.

She loved the sound of his voice. The deep timbre reverberated, causing small tremors of desire to course through her and she held her breath as his gaze locked on to hers. Leaning on muscular forearms, lightly sprinkled with hair, he stretched across the table towards her. Her senses were bathed in the warm, inviting smell of sandalwood. Quietly, his gaze intent, he asked, "Now, tell me about you. What's a beautiful lady doing sitting in a hotel lounge, late in the evening, alone?" His eyes roamed down her body and desire coursed through her. She could do nothing to prevent her nipples beading as his eyes skimmed her chest before returning to focus on her face.

Christ, Chloe. Get a grip of yourself. You would think you had never seen a man before. She chided herself.

"But, I'm not alone." At his small frown, she rushed to quantify her statement, "I'm sitting with you."

He grinned at her attempt to tease him, raising an eyebrow in query he prompted, "Well?"

"Pardon?" Her mind had turned to mush and she couldn't remember his question. She cursed her libido. Why the hell did it have to kick in tonight?

"I said," he was now openly grinning at her, as if he knew that she was flustered, and was amused by her reaction to him, "what are you doing in town?"

"Oh, hmm…sorry. I'm in town for the night as I have an appointment early in the morning."

"You don't live locally then?"

"Well… yes and no." She twirled a long strand of her hair around her fingers.

"I live on the outskirts of London. My appointment is early and rather than have to face the commuter rush it was easier to stay in town overnight." She didn't tell him that the appointment was actually an interview or that her prospective employer had arranged and paid for the hotel room.

"This appointment is important to you?" He was studying her face intently as if her reply really mattered to him. "Business or pleasure?"

She felt herself stiffen in response to his query and had to make a conscious effort to relax. She couldn't go through life thinking every man was like her ex or that every question was fodder for a jealous rage. Even so, she felt defensive. "Does it matter?" she replied quickly.

"No. It doesn't matter." He shook his head slightly, obviously bemused at her response. He was studying her intently, and she shuffled in her chair, uncomfortable that she hadn't answered his question. "I was only making small talk."

She felt mean. He'd meant no harm and she hadn't meant to, but she had probably offended him. Impulsively she stretched her arm across the table, bringing her hand to rest on top of his. He turned his hand and grasped her hand in his own. His hold was firm, but gentle. Mesmerized by the desire in his eyes, she could only sit and watch as he slowly raised her hand to his lips.

"I'm sorry." His tone was quiet, but sincere, as if he was aware that somehow he had upset her.

He had done nothing wrong; he had only been trying to make small talk. His apology filled her with guilt and her conscience forced her to defend him. "What are you sorry for? I'm the one that was rude!"

He brushed off her attempt to apologize, taking all of the blame on himself. "No, I obviously said something that triggered unpleasant memories. I could see it in your eyes."

She was surprised at how perceptive he was and wondered if he ever missed anything.

Releasing her hand, he slapped his forehead. "Ah, now I get it." He grinned at her broadly, his eyes alight with humor. "You're famous, travelling incognito, and you're piqued because I didn't recognize you."

The idea was so absurd she couldn't help but giggle.

"Hardly," she said dryly. What would he say if he realized she was a nobody, so down on her luck she was willing to take a job on a remote island, just to have a roof over her head?

His banter had lightened the mood and she realized how long it had been since anyone had made her laugh. Her spirits felt lighter and she determined that she would make the most of the short time she had with him.

"Your face lights up when you laugh." His eyes roamed her face as though memorizing all her features. "You should do it more often."

"And what makes you think that I don't?"

He shrugged. "Call it intuition. I get the feeling you haven't had a lot to laugh about lately."

No way was she going to discuss her past problems with him. "So... tell me about you. Are you married, do you have family?" She asked, attempting to change the subject.

"You want to know if I'm married, but you don't want to know my name?" He gave her a wicked grin before he threw her own words back at her. "What difference does it make?"

He had her there. She could hardly say 'I don't flirt with married men' without him taking it as some kind of come on.

"Mmm, well... I wouldn't want to be taking up your time if you have a partner or a family waiting up at home for you." She had noticed that he didn't wear a wedding ring, but that meant nothing nowadays.

He was openly grinning at her now and she felt mildly embarrassed. She had made it obvious that she wanted to know if he was single and therefore available.

"You can stop fretting, Angel." He gave her a slow smile. "I'm as free as a bird. No wife, no girlfriend, and no children waiting up for me at home."

The butterflies in her stomach took flight as desire for him soared.

"What would you have said if I was married?" He tipped his head to one side, as he watched her closely.

What could she say? "Probably, goodnight," she murmured softly. "I wouldn't want to hold you up." She would have felt keen disappointment at the loss, but she wasn't going to tell him that.

"A girl with morals and principles. I like that!" His eyes were alight with pleasure and she felt inordinately pleased with herself as she basked in his approval.

They passed a pleasant half hour chatting generally about theatre shows on in London and places they had visited. At her insistence, they avoided personal topics and he knew no more than she was in town for the night and that she had an appointment the following morning.

No matter how devastatingly sexy she found him, she still refused to give her name. The desire in his eyes was obvious and she hadn't yet decided whether or not she would accept the promise they offered. She was tempted. What girl wouldn't be? If he didn't have her name and no way of contacting her again after the night was over, she could walk away without entanglements.

It was getting late and she was conscious of the fact that she needed to get a good night's sleep in order to be at her best for her interview in the morning, but she was reluctant to draw the evening to a close. She was having fun. He was an intelligent and entertaining conversationalist. When his opinion on a play or a film they had both seen, differed from her own, he would debate good humoredly with her. Not once did he belittle her ideas. It had been so long since she'd been able to express her own opinions without fear of being mocked and doing so felt good. For the first time in months, she felt light hearted and relaxed, euphoric almost.

If he made her feel this good just talking, how good would he make her feel if he took her to bed? The thought alone had her insides trembling and she squirmed in her seat as her internal muscles pulsed. Damn, her panties were wet now. What would she say if he asked if he could spend the night with her? Did she dare accept? She caught herself looking at his hands. They were large with long fingers; his nails were square cut and looked immaculate. What would it feel like to have those hands on her skin, cupping her breasts? Her nipples beaded in anticipation and moisture pooled at the juncture of her thighs as her wayward thoughts caused her to tremble in anticipation.

If she was successful at her interview then she would be out of circulation for a while as the position she had applied for was located on a remote island. It could be a long time before she had the opportunity to have male company and she doubted she would ever meet anyone as gorgeous as this man. Surely it couldn't be wrong to enjoy just one night of passion before she cloistered herself away?

Taking a deep breath, she closed her eyes briefly as she clenched her thighs together. She had to get herself under control. Maybe he didn't want to spend a night with her. She was surprised at the disappointment that thought caused. She cast a quick look at her watch. It was nearly midnight and she really must be thinking of calling the evening to a close soon. She realized that her internal thoughts had caused a lull in their conversation and cursed herself when she realized he was watching her quizzically. She felt herself blush and hoped he hadn't guessed what she was thinking.

"Feeling tired?" He asked.

"A little…" she answered, and then wondered why she'd said that. Now he would be thinking she wanted to call it a night and she wasn't ready to let him go just yet.

Xander looked towards the sound of breaking glass and noticed the bankers were starting to get rowdy. Reluctantly, he decided it was time to leave the bar before things got out of hand. Despite all his requests she had refused to reveal her name or hand over her phone number.

What was she hiding? There had to be some reason she refused to acknowledge the chemistry between them. He had not been the only one to experience the pull of sexual attraction, he assured himself, it was definitely mutual. The signs of her arousal had been unmistakable. Even so, he had the uncomfortable feeling that she wasn't going to give in to it. He was surprised at the disappointment that crashed over him with that thought. Why didn't she want to see him again? They were both free agents, over the age of consent, with nothing to stop them indulging their mutual attraction. What was she afraid of?

Rising from his seat, he gave a mocking bow as he held out his hand to her. "Well then, Angel. I would consider it an honor to see you safely to your room."

She collected her purse from under the table and rose slowly before putting her hand in his. He was elated at her tacit acceptance of his offer. Maybe, just maybe, there was a chance she would invite him to stay. He had enjoyed his time with her. She was intelligent and quick-witted. It had taken a little coaxing to bring her out of herself. At first, she had been wary, her opinions expressed stiltedly as though she expected rebuke but when she had finally let go and relaxed he had watched in amazement as she blossomed before his eyes. Her face was very expressive and betrayed her emotions. She would never make a poker player, because her eyes gave away her every thought. *Those same eyes would make her a great submissive though. She would be so easy to read, so easy to pleasure.* He was forced to bite the inside of his cheek in order to stifle the moan of desire that thought conjured up.

He held her hand as they crossed the foyer to the lifts in silence. When they entered the lift, she slowly withdrew her hand from his, as if she was reluctant to let him go. She leaned against the back wall, wrapped her arms around her middle and studied her shoes as if she suddenly found them fascinating. The way she nibbled on her lower lip made him wonder whether she was worried that he was going to pounce on her. Maybe she was right to be worried. He was struggling to control the urge to place his mouth over hers and soothe the spot she'd nibbled.

She was a mass of contradictions, a puzzle he needed to solve. With the resources he had at his disposal, it wouldn't take him long to find out everything he needed to know about her. One phone call was all it would take to find out her name, and once he knew that he could run a full background check. He didn't want to go down that route though. He was still hoping that she would volunteer the information, thereby indicating that she wanted to see him again.

As the lift bumped to a halt at her floor, she lifted her head and met his gaze. His eyes locked onto hers, and he found himself holding his breath as he waited to see what her next move would be. She was as still as a rabbit caught in the glare of headlights.

The lift doors opened and she swung her gaze towards the low-lit corridor. With eye contact now broken, his tension eased and he let go of the breath he'd been holding.

"Come on, Sleepyhead." He held out his hand towards her, "Time to get you into bed."

He kept his free hand anchored to her lower back as they walked silently down the corridor to her room. The lights in the corridor were set low and the thick carpet underfoot allowed no sound from their footsteps. When they arrived at her door, she turned her back to him as she rummaged in her purse searching for her key. He noticed that her hand was unsteady as she struggled to insert the key into the lock. When he put a steadying hand on her shoulder, she jumped as though startled. He reached over and took the key from her trembling fingers, opened the door, and handed the key back to her.

He was uncertain whether she was nervous or trembling in anticipation. He prayed it was the latter. He had every intention of kissing her and finding out. She had been driving him mad for the last hour and he was desperate to taste her, even if it was just a goodnight kiss at the door.

She straightened her shoulders and he heard her take a deep breath. Then she turned once again to face him. She was suddenly formal as she extended her hand. "Thank you for the company. It's never very pleasant to sit alone in a hotel and I enjoyed our chat."

Shit.... he hadn't seen that coming and he was surprised at the depth of disappointment that crashed over him. He needed to think fast and find something to break the sudden tension between them. Aware that she couldn't see him as a threat if he wanted to see her again, he decided to try a little humor. Clutching his hands to his chest, over his heart, he presented her with a crestfallen face. "Do I not even get a goodnight kiss?" he asked, as he struggled to contain his disappointment.

She laughed gently at him, her eyes aglow with mischief and he sighed with relief, grateful that she appeared to appreciate his sense of humor.

"Oh, I think I can manage that." She tilted her head to one side and he was captivated by her lopsided smile.

She stood on tiptoe and appeared to be aiming for his cheek as she leaned toward him. No way was he going to settle for a peck when he had been burning for a taste of her. He turned his head and caught her lips, slowly caressing them with his own, savoring the taste of the woman and the drink she had consumed. He needed more and he pulled her unresisting body closer, enfolding her against his chest, as he gave into his craving. He ran the tip of his tongue along the seam of her mouth and she opened giving him access, allowing him to plunder and stroke her tongue with his own. Her arms crept up and around his neck in apparent surrender. He struggled to keep his kiss light and teasing, aware of the need to tread gently. She was still skittish, as though unaware of her appeal, and the last thing he wanted to do was frighten her.

He couldn't get her close enough. He skimmed his hands down her sides and loved the delicious way she trembled when he brought her up against his erection. He cupped her bottom firmly enjoying the moans and whimpers of pleasure emanating from her throat. The sound of her desire fed his passion and he ground himself against her, letting her know how much he wanted her. Even as they kissed, he was aware of her hands digging into his shoulders as she clenched her fingers and tugged on his shirt encouraging him closer.

How long they stood necking like teenagers in the hallway he couldn't say, but when he raised his head, they were both panting heavily and her eyes were slumberous with desire.

"Invite me in," he growled, desperate now to bury himself within her body.

Christ, he was acting like a horny schoolboy. He could normally control his impulses. What the hell was it about this woman that fired him up so quickly? He fought to get himself back under control.

"Angel?" He questioned. He felt slightly nervous as he awaited her answer. He wasn't used to having to persuade women into his bed. He tried to appear calm as he didn't want to unsettle her, but his stomach muscles were clenched tight as he waited on her response.

She barely nodded her head, but it was all the encouragement he needed. He bent down and hooked an arm behind her knees as he picked her up and hastily stepped into her small hotel suite, kicking the door shut behind them. He strode into the bedroom, pleased to see the traditional old-fashioned bed. It was the ideal type of bed with lots of anchor points should he want to tie her up. He discounted that idea almost immediately. There was no way he could indulge those fantasies tonight. He placed her in the center of the bed as if she was made of fragile china instead of flesh and blood.

As he followed her down, he lay on his side and gathered her into his arms. Her arms came up between them to grab at his shirt as she attempted to undo his buttons. It appeared she was as eager as he to get skin to skin and he loved her enthusiasm. Eager as he was to join his body with hers, he needed to slow things down. If he was only going to have this one night with her, he wanted to make every minute count. It was time that he took control.

"Not so fast, Angel." He leaned forward capturing her hands and, pinning her arms above her head. "My turn first. I want to savor unwrapping you."

He rolled over and straddled her hips holding her in position while he peeled her hands away from his chest.

The soft moan of desire she emitted was her only response, but it was all the encouragement he needed. He transferred both of her wrists to one hand. Still holding her arms above her head he looked at her hair fanned out on the pillows, and thought about the ways he could use it to hold her and control her response. He reminded himself that this was a one night only event, unlikely to be repeated, so his imagination would have to suffice.

He bent to trace the shell of her ear with his tongue and was delighted when she gave a small shiver at his touch. He continued to lick and stroke down the length of her neck, biting gently at the juncture of her shoulder. She gasped and twisted below him obviously enjoying his ministrations. He licked the spot to soothe where he'd nipped and his free hand roamed down the side of her body before skimming under her top. He stopped to draw circles around her belly button causing her to giggle and wriggle beneath him. He relished the friction against his erection for a moment, before making his way upwards to her luscious breasts. He felt her heart rate increase as he molded his hand over one soft breast encased in lace. Her nipple had formed a tight bud and was trying to poke through its covering. As she arched her back pushing her breast into his hand, he emitted a low groan of appreciation at her response. He was eager to see her naked and in her full glory. His mouth watered at the thought of sucking on her pouting nipples.

Still straddled across her thighs he lifted her into a sitting position, so that they sat chest to chest. Her eyes flared with desire as he swiftly discarded the soft cotton top she wore. Unlike the Mediterranean lovers he had taken in the past, her skin was pale, almost translucent. As he trailed his tongue slowly across the swell of her breast, luxuriating in the pearl like quality, she closed her eyes and let out a soft moan. She took his breath away. As he let go of her arms and threw her blouse over his shoulder, she collapsed back onto the bed, arms still above her head. Her back arched pushing her breasts towards him. Her lush breasts were barely contained by the delicate peach colored lace bra that almost matched her skin tone. He couldn't wait a moment longer to taste her. He bent and kissed her hard as he slipped a hand swiftly behind her back to unclip her bra. He was surprised when she giggled before informing him that the fastening was at the front. Shit, he felt like a novice. It was no wonder she was amused.

He wanted so badly to release his inner demon. The thought of her tied and spread eagled on the bed as he brought her to climax caused his erection to throb. He fought back the urge to make demands she couldn't hope to meet tonight. He doubted she had ever experimented with the lifestyle and tonight wasn't the time to introduce her to it. He had a feeling one night with her would not be enough which meant he needed to persuade her to see him again if he wanted the opportunity to do all the things he fantasized about doing with her.

He shook his head at her and growled, "I'm not a man to tease, Angel." He grabbed her hands and positioned them around the rails of the bedstead stretching them high above her head.

"Keep your hands there, don't move them," he told her firmly. In an effort to soften his command, he bent to whisper in her ear, "I'll make you pay for laughing at me. I'm going to taste every delicious inch of you. You'll be begging for release by the time I'm finished."

His excitement spiked on her husky, "Oh yes?"

He looked at her incredulous, had she really questioned his ability? Well, she had thrown down the gauntlet and he wasn't a man to refuse a challenge, especially one issued by a slip of a girl.

He unclipped the front of her bra and her bountiful breasts spilled out to be captured by his hands. He palmed them firmly testing their weight and fullness before rubbing his thumbs across her nipples. She had dusky pink areolas and her nipples were large, firm and stood at attention with her desire. She moaned softly as he continued to stroke them and he loved that she was so sensitive to his touch. She gasped when he suddenly bent to draw one into his mouth and she pushed the back of her head into the pillow and arched her back. She was panting softly as she offered her breast up to his mouth, encouraging him, as he circled her nipple with his tongue. He laved it thoroughly before he sucked it between his lips and gave her a gentle nip with his teeth, which caused her to moan loudly. He knew she would feel the pull on her nipple right down to her womb and he was rewarded when her hips started to undulate gently under him.

He transferred his mouth to her other nipple to give it the same attention. At the same time, he pinched hard on the first nipple which was still wet from his mouth. She moaned aloud and arched off the bed, thrusting her pelvis up toward him. He was pleased that she seemed to be enjoying the slight pain and he registered the knowledge that she enjoyed a little pain with her pleasure. The idea excited him.

He kissed his way down her flat stomach, pausing to twirl his tongue around the inside of her belly button. He slid further down her legs and began to push her loose pants down. She came to his aid, lifting her bottom off the bed so that he could slide them down and over her hips.

He unfolded his long frame from the bed and swiftly yanked the wide legged cotton pants off her legs. Her eyes popped open and, with a look of surprise on her face, she watched as he tossed the pants aside. He paused a moment to admire the view of her wearing nothing but the open bra and a matching lace thong. The sight was enough to make his mouth salivate. He noted with pleasure that she still held tightly to the bedrails and had not removed her hands, as he'd instructed. She could follow instructions and he liked that.

She gave him a soft smile, which he took as encouragement to continue his sensual assault. He took a deep breath as he fought to maintain control, now more than before he was conscious of his cock as it strained for release. Patience. Her pleasure first. He reminded himself.

His shirt was hanging open and he watched her gaze travel the length of his body, slowly perusing his chest and following the line of hair down over his abs to where it vanished into his pants. When she licked her lips slowly, he almost came undone. As she watched, he discarded his shirt and trousers, toed off his socks and shoes, kicking them free before he climbed back onto the bed in his boxers. She watched him but said nothing. The sultry look in her eyes told him as clearly as any words would have that she liked what she saw. When her eyes skimmed across the front of his tented boxers, she nibbled her bottom lip and moaned softly. The sound of her pleasure reverberated through him like a caress, and he promised himself he would draw many more moans from her before the night was over. He would make her beg for her release.

He picked up one leg and started slowly sucking each toe as his hands caressed around the arch of her foot and up her calf. She moaned aloud as his tongue lapped around each toe in turn, her thigh muscles tensed but she did not try to pull away. As he continued to caress her with slow circular motions, she relaxed and opened her legs wider, encouraging his progress toward her pussy. He worked his way slowly up the length of her leg, kissing inch by delicious inch until he reached her inner thigh. He could smell her arousal and see the darker patch of lace where she had soaked her panties. He slipped his fingers under the edge of the lace and stroked her softly, tempting her with what was to come. As he withdrew, she gave a little moan of dismay and thrust her pelvis towards him.

He was determined to deny himself the taste of her for just a little while longer, even though his own craving was crying out to be appeased.

He stroked over the front of her panties as he gently teased her by withholding the pressure he knew she craved. He was rewarded when her breath hitched and she started to pant softly. When she moaned, he moved on. He traveled down her other leg to her toes, repeating the kissing and sucking process he had lavished on the other foot. He reveled in the control he had over her as she writhed slowly on the bed, her hands still obediently wrapped around the headboard.

He knelt between her splayed legs and worked his way back up toward her core. He slowly stroked a hand up each leg until his hands met in the middle at her mound. He cupped her gently, stroking her slick folds through the lace of her panties. He gave enough pressure to give her pleasure but not enough to let her cum. With her eyes closed, she tossed her head side to side as she whimpered and made kittenish noises at the back of her throat. The sound of her passion increased his own desire and his erection throbbed painfully within the confines of his shorts. His stomach muscles tensed with need as he registered how wet and ready she was for him. He wanted to bury himself within her heat, but more than that, he wanted to make their coming together feel so good that she wouldn't be able to refuse to see him again.

Her hips rocked up and down against his hand trying to increase the pressure as she strived to reach her release. Keeping one hand in place cupping her mound, he raised up and over her. He kissed her hard before demanding, "Open your eyes."

Her eyes flew open and she stared at him as he'd instructed, "Keep your eyes open and on me. I want to look into your eyes when you cum."

She gasped loudly and her lashes swept down to cover her eyes. He'd obviously shocked her by his forthright demand, but he didn't feel sorry. Instead, he felt irritated that her previous lovers had obviously allowed her to hide from her own passionate nature. *Had they not realized what a prize she was?* Compulsion to watch her reaction when he finally brought her to climax drove him on. "Open your eyes."

She held his gaze and lay so still he was sure she was holding her breath. When he winked and said, "That's the price of your orgasm," she exhaled sharply. To his delight, she blushed and he watched the flush travel down her neck and over her magnificent breasts. Unable to resist he followed the trail with his tongue until he reached the apex of her thighs.

He lifted his head to look at her, "Eyes on me," he commanded.

When she raised her head slightly to look directly into his eyes, he grasped the lace of her thong and tore it apart and away from her body. She gasped, whether in shock or delight he wasn't sure, but as his head dipped between her legs and his tongue probed the length of her wet slit her gasp turned to sighs of pleasure.

He brought his hands up to push her legs wider apart as the tip of his tongue sought out and teased her clit. He placed his hands under her bottom to lift and open her further as he continued to stroke and tease. He watched her steadily until she let her head fall back and closed her eyes. He stopped teasing and waited.

Looking puzzled, she opened her eyes to look at him. On meeting his gaze, her blue eyes widened in wonder and held a hint of desperation and intense longing. As soon as her gaze connected with his he returned to the task at hand. The taste of her was like nectar and he couldn't get enough. He lapped at the sweetness between her slick folds. Every now and then, he swept his tongue across her clit making her hips jerk as she cried out her need.

He pushed a finger inside her and felt her body start to tremble. He curled his finger seeking out her G-spot as he laved her clit. He burrowed deeper and sucked her clit gently between his lips all the time keeping his eyes on her face. When she once again closed her eyes, he immediately stopped what he was doing and waited. She groaned aloud, giving voice to her frustration then she opened her eyes to gaze pleadingly at him. He said nothing but steadily returned her gaze. He was unable to deny his nature any longer. His dominance was coming to the fore. He wasn't happy she had closed her eyes for a second time. He arched an eyebrow conveying his displeasure and continued to stare her down. If it came to a battle of wills, she had no chance of winning. Unable to hold his stare she cast her eyes down and surveyed him through half open eyes. She took a deep breath and gave a small nod of her head. At her silent agreement to his terms, he threw her a broad smile to convey his pleasure at her acceptance of his rules. Once again, he dipped his head to taste the cream she had produced.

With two fingers buried inside her, he watched her face closely. He brought her nearer and nearer to climax as he stroked her harder and faster. All the while, his tongue licked up and down the length of her. She was climbing to her peak, her body bathed in a light coating of perspiration and her back arched off the bed at each swipe his tongue made across her clit.

"Please.... Oh please."

Shit, she begged so sweetly!

Her pussy walls clenched and squeezed his fingers, and he longed to be buried inside her. First though he wanted to watch her cum. She still held his gaze but now her eyes were begging, pleading for the release her body wanted. He wanted to watch her go up in flames. He took her rigid little clit in his mouth and sucked it hard between his lips before he proceeded to nibble gently as he rocked his fingers inside her. She bucked and thrashed on the bed. Her husky cries of need echoed around the room and he wanted to reward her for the passion she revealed. He held her clit between his lips and stroked its length with his tongue causing her to moan and wriggle against his tongue. When she reached the pinnacle of her need, he bit down quite firmly to send her screaming into her climax. Her body went rigid and arched head to foot, before she collapsed sweetly flushed, limp and trembling on the bed.

He could wait no longer. Kicking off his boxers, he picked her up quickly and turned her over. He shifted her backwards, bringing her to a kneeling position. One hand on her back, he pushed her shoulders lower and entered her swiftly from behind. He could not hold back his moan of pleasure, as his cock was bathed in the warm juices of her cum and held tight by the sweet spasms still wracking her body.

He had not intended to take her hard, but the sight of her on her knees with her backside in the air was more than he could take and he grasped her hips tightly as he pounded into her hard and fast.

He wrapped an arm around her front where his fingers once again sought and found her clit. He rubbed her gently, spreading her juices along her crease, as he continued to pound into her from behind. He bent and nipped her nape and whispered in her ear, "Now, baby girl, I need you to cum again. I want to feel your cream flooding around my cock!"

In the lifestyle he enjoyed, Doms often taught their submissive to cum on command. She moaned obviously excited by the thought of cumming again and pushed herself back against him. The mewling sounds she made in the back of her throat drove him on. He stroked her rigid little clit, unable to suppress his own moan of desire as her internal muscles tightened around his shaft. He didn't think he could hold on much longer. His balls were heavy and tight. He was ready to explode when she finally climaxed around him, flooding him with her juices. The strong spasms which wracked her core and tightened around his length sent his good intentions to the wind. His ejaculation was so powerful it took him by surprise and he struggled to keep them both upright as her pussy muscles pulsed around him.

They collapsed on the bed in a tangle of limbs. She was still trembling with the aftermath of her climax when she turned toward him. He enfolded her in his arms as she rained small breathless kisses across his chest. She snuggled up against him, a gesture so trusting he was taken aback considering she had refused to give him her name. He stroked and caressed her back and the swell of her hip, loving the feel of her soft skin. He cupped her hip and pulled her closer as he thought about not seeing her. The very idea of not being able to hold her like this again unsettled him and he instinctively threaded a hand through her hair as he held her to him. He realized that he wasn't ready to let her go. He continued to hold her close as he pondered a solution. Her head rested against his chest and her fingers entwined with his chest hair as her breathing calmed. Lost in his own thoughts, it was a moment or two before he realized that her breathing had deepened and she had fallen asleep.

The night was nearly over and he was running out of time. She had mentioned something about an appointment in the morning as her reason for being in town. He needed to get a move on if he wanted to carry out his plans before she checked out in the morning. If he was going to find out everything he needed to know before she vanished out of his life, he needed to get out of bed. He needed to call his chief of security and get him to find out exactly who she was. Once he had a name, he would be able to get all the information he needed within hours. By the time she awoke, he would know everything he needed to know. He eased her back under the covers, amused at the small murmur of protest she gave before she turned over and burrowed into the quilt. It looked like he wasn't the only one who was feeling the pull between them. Her small protest gave him hope.

On shaky legs, he made his way to the bathroom to dispose of his condom, only then realizing that they had not used one. He cursed himself for being an idiot. He had gotten so carried away that he had forgotten to sheath himself, something he had never done before.

His lack of care shook him to the core; it was unlike him to be so careless. Never before had he made love to a woman without ensuring protection. He watched her sleep apparently unaware of his presence. He had no choice; he justified his decision to himself. He had to find out exactly who she was. He needed to keep her close, at least until he found out whether there were going to be consequences to his oversight.

The night was nearly over. He needed to get a move on if he wanted to carry out his plans before she checked out of the hotel in the morning. She was exhausted and still asleep when he finished dressing.

He sat on the edge of bed and leaned over to kiss her. Even in her sleep, her lips clung to his.

"Angel, I'm leaving now."

"Okay," she murmured sleepily.

"That's all you can say?" She wasn't falling over herself to arrange to see him again or to give him her contact details and he was disappointed that she wasn't as keen as he was to explore the chemistry between them further. "Do you want to give me your name and number before I leave?"

Half asleep, she shook her head negatively. "No names. We agreed."

He felt like he'd taken a blow to the stomach. In amazement, he watched as she rolled over onto her side and went straight back to sleep. His jaw tensed and he bit the inside of his cheek to stop himself rousing her to argue with her. He wanted to rant at her stubborn stance, but she needed her sleep and he needed to go and put his plans in place before he ran out of time. It didn't really matter that she wouldn't divulge her name, he would have all the information he needed soon enough but, to his surprise, it hurt. He had really wanted her to want to continue what they had started. He really didn't like the thought of setting investigators on her case, but she had left him no option.

She had made it plain at the start of the evening that she did not want to swap contact details. He hadn't liked it, but he had agreed to her 'no names' game at the time. Now, he had every intention of finding out exactly who she was. He was determined that he would see her again, after all she may now be carrying his child.

He booked an alarm call with reception on her behalf and let himself quietly out of the hotel room. On his way to the lift, he pulled out his mobile and called Giles. His head of security was now based in London, in order to be closer to him if needed.

"Meet me at the office, pronto!" He bit out, "I've got an urgent job for you."

Chapter Three

The shrill ringing of the telephone on the nightstand woke Chloe with a start. As she reached to answer, she groaned as she felt the pull on muscles not used for a long time.

She thanked reception for the alarm call she didn't remember booking, and flushed as she spotted her torn thong and some bank notes beside the phone. She couldn't believe he had left money to replace the panties. It made her feel cheap, like he had paid for her favors.

Maybe he had, the thought flashed through her mind. She'd been brought up to believe that nice girls didn't do one-night stands, but she could feel no shame. Instead, she basked in the euphoria she had felt after his love making.

Now that he was gone, she regretted her decision to keep her identity secret. Her 'no names' game had seemed like a good idea at the time, but now she realized that because of that decision she'd never see him again.

She lay back on the bed and immersed herself in the memories of his lovemaking. She had allowed him to control her body and had luxuriated in the way he had played her. After Nick, she had never thought she would let any man have control over her again, but this had felt so different. She had felt adored, as if he controlled her for her pleasure and not just for his own. At no time had she felt manipulated and she sighed with regret that she had let him get away.

There would be no way he could find her, even if he wanted to. She was only in town for the night, and the hotel room was being paid for by the unknown Xander; the man she was having an interview with later that morning.

Chloe needed to get the position she was being interviewed for. Getting the job would allow her to move away from the area and avoid Nick. Nevertheless, she still cursed herself for being stupid enough to let tall, dark and gorgeous get away.

She had two hours to get ready for her interview and she used the time to shower and dress. She donned a suit, formal, smart but still very feminine; the neat navy jacket nipped in at the waist and the slim fitting skirt finished just above her knee. Under the jacket, she wore a cream silk blouse and finished off her ensemble with neat court shoes. With her hair swept up into a neat bun and a minimum of makeup she was pleased with the overall result. She double-checked to make sure she had all her certificates and references from previous employers in her briefcase in case they were requested.

Unsure what to expect she presented herself at the hotel's front desk as she'd been instructed. The desk clerk directed her toward a small conference suite at the side entrance to the hotel. She was met by a very efficient man, who introduced himself as Mr. Doumas's assistant. She was to wait in the small reception area until she was called in to be interviewed.

Lost in her thoughts and not paying attention as she should have been, she was taken unaware when the assistant came back to escort her into her interview.

"Mr. Doumas will see you now," he smiled warmly. "Please go through." He indicated the double doors at the opposite side of the room.

Head held high and trying to hide her nerves she made her way across the room, knocking politely at the door before entering. The room, though well appointed, was impersonal as belied a hotel conference suite. The occupant at the head of the table had his chair turned away from the door facing towards the large picture window on the opposite wall. From what she could see he appeared to be studying a file he held in his hands.

"Please close the door and take a seat. I'll be with you in a minute." The voice was deep and rich, with a slight accent. It spilled over her like liquid chocolate, warm and comforting, vaguely familiar. She put that niggle to the back of her mind; she needed to concentrate on her interview. She needed this job to escape from Nick.

Xander deliberately kept his back to the room. He wanted to wait until she had seated herself before he turned to look at her. He needed to see her reaction to his presence. His stomach knotted with tension as he wondered how she would take his appearance. He would have sworn that last night she had no clue as to who he was, but as soon as Giles had returned from the hotel with the name of his mystery lover, he had realized that she was a potential candidate that he would be interviewing.

He couldn't help but wonder if she had known his identity while keeping her own hidden. If so, what was her motivation? Was she another freeloader looking for a wealthy benefactor, or had she hoped that sleeping with him would guarantee her the post?

Disappointment crashed over him. He was sick of women trying to get close to him because of his wealth. He had enjoyed his night with her, had convinced himself that she was shy and insecure. Now he wondered if she had deceived him.

He gripped the file in his hands, struggling to control the rage he could feel bubbling inside. There was no way he would let her make a fool of him. After the media debacle Marie had caused, he had to be ultra cautious. He was determined not to put his family through that kind of publicity again.

He closed the file and released a deep sigh. He would know soon enough. Chloe's face was so expressive, he'd be able to read her reaction. The ability to read her easily had been one of the things that had drawn him to her.

He took several deep breaths as he fought to compose himself. When he turned around, he wanted her to have no hint that she had affected him. He needed to be the one in control of their meeting.

He spun his chair and immediately focused on her face. Was she surprised to see him? He cast a quick look over her, taking in the professional suit and the careful makeup. She looked beautiful and totally composed. Bitch. He clenched his jaw to hold back the curse. Her face betrayed no emotion and he was unable to read her. She had looked neither surprised nor dismayed at the sight of him.

Shit! Why couldn't he read her? He wondered if she had deliberately played him for a fool. Whatever she was up to, she was a darn good actress. He had been totally fooled by her innocent and shy persona the previous evening. He slapped her file down on the table, taken aback at the anger simmering through his veins.

"Well, Chloe, looks like we meet again!" His tone was mocking.

Chloe was stunned, unable to think straight. She had held herself motionless, almost rigid with shock, as she endured his silent appraisal. Could her luck get any worse? Her prospective employer and her one-night stand were one and the same.

Last night she had basked in his approval, this morning he was looking at her with disdain. She couldn't understand why he looked so angry. Her stomach churned and she felt nauseous as it hit her that she had blown her chance of getting the job. She cursed herself for her actions the previous night. What the hell had possessed her?

He was silently awaiting her reply. He looked puzzled and his eyes searched her face as if he was trying to read her thoughts. Pinned to the spot, she inwardly squirmed. The swine was enjoying her discomfort! Unable to meet his gaze she posed her response to the window over his shoulder.

"You're Xander Doumas I presume?" She flushed, embarrassed to her soul.

From the corner of her eye, she caught the nod he gave in reply to her question. Christ the man knew every inch of her intimately and she had to ask him to confirm his name. She wriggled in her chair, mortified.

He continued to look at her. His gaze was probing and she felt trapped by his silent study.

She bit her lip in consternation and would have sworn she heard him growl low and deep in his throat. Her gaze swung back to his face; she could do nothing more than look at him as passion flared in his eyes. His gaze was now fixed on her swollen bottom lip.

Her shoulders slumped in defeat, as she accepted that there was no way she was going to be offered the position she had applied for. She took a deep breath and closed her eyes breaking eye contact with him. She couldn't think straight when he looked at her like that. Her best course of action, to save them both from further embarrassment, would be to terminate the interview.

Decision made, she rose from her chair. Holding her slim briefcase in front of her like a shield, she backed away from the conference table dismayed at how events had turned out.

"Well, Mr.…" she hated herself for stumbling on his name, "Mr. Doumas," she spoke rapidly, her voice shaky with nerves, "as there doesn't seem to be a lot of point in going through with this interview under the circumstances I'm…"

"Sit down!" The look he gave her was uncompromising. His tone was harsh and brooked no argument.

She looked at him in disbelief; surely, he didn't intend to go through with this farce. He hadn't moved from the chair, but he was now leaning forward across the table, pointing to the chair she had just vacated. "Sit."

Who the hell did he think he was talking to? She wasn't about to obey a command she'd normally expect to hear directed at a dog!

She had just survived one controlling relationship. She had let Nick speak to her like that, and it had been a mistake. She wasn't about to let anyone else control her. She shook her head slowly, and continued backing away from the table.

He rose, towering over the table as he walked slowly around it. He stopped short of her and casually hitched one hip against the table with his arms crossed over his broad chest. Not once did he take his eyes off her. She couldn't deny the delicious tingle throughout her body at the sight of him. He made no move towards her, just stayed where he was; half perched on the corner of the table. The position pulled his pants tight and showed off his muscular thighs. Memories of the previous evening came rushing back and a flood of longing nearly overwhelmed her. Her own carnal thoughts caused her to blush and brought a sardonic smirk to his mouth; bastard, he knew exactly what effect he was having on her.

However, he was no longer the attentive lover of the previous night; now he looked like an employer about to give a reprimand. The pulse at the side of his jaw beat a rapid tattoo and his eyes were cold. He looked like he was fighting to control his temper. Her heartbeat increased as she wondered what his next move would be. She flung a hasty glance over her shoulder gauging the distance to the door.

"If you don't sit down now and do as you are told," he said conversationally, as if he saw nothing out of the ordinary in their circumstance, "I will put you over my knee and spank you for willful disobedience."

She was aghast, surely she had misheard him. "You can't say that to an employee. It's harassment. It's assault." Her breath caught in her throat and her heart raced. "You wouldn't dare!"

"You're not an employee yet, and, yes I would!" He replied; seeming not at all fazed by her outburst.

Her legs started to tremble and she could feel her heart pounding in her chest. Was he serious? She studied him for a second or two trying to assess the risk, but she no longer trusted her own judgment. He had made no further move towards her but a flashback to the first time Nick had raised his hand to her, exploded through her consciousness. Bitterness at the mistreatment she had suffered, hardened her resolve. She refused to become a victim again and she did not intend to hang around and give him the chance to carry out his threat.

She spun on her heel and bolted for the door, adrenalin and fear pounding through her veins. She felt little relief as she stepped into the corridor and slammed the door behind her. She walked as quickly as she could without drawing unwanted attention as she headed toward the bank of elevators at the end of corridor. Panic beat a steady rhythm in her chest as she endeavored not to break into a run. Keeping her gaze focused on the elevators, she managed to avoid turning around to see if he was following her, but she listened intently for any sound behind.

She didn't know him well enough to know how he was going to react. Would he follow her? Would he carry out his threat? Her mind was racing as she mentally ran through the possibilities. How long did she have to get back to her room, collect her bags and get as far away from him as possible?

Xander was stunned and unable to move for a second or two. What the hell? She had looked terrified and he berated himself for being a bastard as he launched himself across the room. He threw the door open and saw her retreating back.

"Angel, stop!"

She cast a quick, panic-struck glance over her shoulder before increasing her speed down the corridor, each step taking her further away from him. Shit! What a bloody mess.

He was going to have to follow her and try to put things right, but there was no way he was going to be caught running through the hotel after her. The hotel staff would love that spectacle, no doubt, but he was determined not to become fodder for the gossip mill again. He stayed poised in the doorway, ignoring the speculative glances flung in his direction by passers by, until she turned the corridor.

Once she was out of sight he pulled the door shut behind him and set off after her, his gait measured and controlled, he stalked her shadow. Had his quip about spanking set off the panic that had caused her to run?

As he made his determined way through the corridors of the hotel, he thought back to her file. He recalled mention of a court case where she had been the victim of assault.

He was an idiot! He had threatened to spank her. In the circumstances, it was no wonder she had run. She wouldn't have seen spanking as a form of erotic foreplay, she would have seen it as a threatened assault. No wonder she had taken off like a scared rabbit. He reached the elevators just as the doors closed and he stood to watch as the light indicated a stop at her floor. Frustrated at the delay, he raked his fingers through his hair as he awaited the arrival of the next elevator. He was full of self-loathing and sick to his stomach at the thought of how distressed she must be. He doubted she'd willingly give him the chance to apologize.

On the way up in the elevator, he tossed around ideas, trying to figure out the best way to approach her. He wondered which option would give him the better chance of getting through to her. He wavered between a formal business approach or, his favored option, of misunderstood lover.

She saw him as a threat. Pain tore through his gut and his stomach muscles tightened at the thought. He couldn't let her walk away thinking he had intended to harm her. He couldn't let her walk away, period. He had to find a way to get through to her, to convince her he meant her no harm. Christ, he had never hurt a woman in his life, well not without their prior consent.

Looking at his reflection in the elevator mirror, he made a conscious effort to relax. If she saw him now with his fists clenched, the tension throughout his body apparent in every line, he would frighten the life out of her. He had to persuade her he was harmless and to do that he needed to look the part.

The elevator doors opened, depositing him at her floor. Determined to check that she was okay, his long stride soon ate up the distance to her room. At the door he hesitated, unsure of himself and the reception he was about to receive. That in itself was something new. He couldn't remember a time when he'd had to strive to gain the attention of a woman; they were normally all too eager to get to know him. He admitted to himself that she didn't know him well enough yet to trust him. He was going to have to muster up every ounce of charm he possessed if he was going to persuade her to give him another chance.

Upon reaching her door, he took a few moments to calm himself. He heard drawers slamming and could imagine her panic as she raced around collecting her belongings. Satisfied that she hadn't already flown, he took a deep breath, and knocked on her door. His rap on the door was met by silence and in his minds eye he could envision her frozen on the spot. Shit!

"Angel," he called through the door. "Come on, Angel. Open the door and let me in."

"Go away." Her tremulous plea rocked him. She sounded like she was crying and he cursed himself under his breath.

"Please, Angel." He leaned against the door, talking to her through the woodwork. "I'm sorry I frightened you. Honestly, sweetheart," he lowered his tone, "you have nothing to be afraid of. Please let me in. I need to see that you're okay."

He needed to make things right between them. What the hell had he been thinking of back in the conference room? He grimaced as he remembered what he'd been thinking, that she had known of his identity the previous evening while keeping him ignorant of her own. He'd been thinking that maybe she was an opportunist out to ensnare him because of his wealth.

The heavy feeling in his gut felt a lot like shame. He was guilty of making her pay for another's sins and the knowledge shook him and made him question his sense of fair play. He hadn't given her a chance; he'd judged and found her guilty. He could only pray she would give him a chance to make that up to her. All thoughts that she may have been aware of his identity were now forgotten. If he didn't get through to her, convince her she would be safe with him, he was never going to see her again. The thought was untenable and he racked his brain to come up with something to convince her she was safe.

There was no response from beyond the closed door, but some sixth sense told him that she was listening to him.

"Angel?" He received no response.

"Chloe." He tried again, this time using her given name. It felt odd because in his mind she would always be 'Angel'.

"Please open the door," he coaxed against the wood. "We need to talk."

Listening intently as he leaned against the door, he heard her hiccup, before she replied tremulously, "I don't think we have anything to say to each other."

She was definitely crying and he mentally cursed himself to hell and back for causing her tears. He exhaled a long slow breath, striving to remain patient, when he really wanted to break the door down and take her in his arms. It was his own fault he was in this position. It had been his stupid threat to spank her for willful disobedience that had sent her running for cover.

"Angel. Please," he was reduced to begging. "Just open the door and let me in. If it will make you feel safer you can call for a member of the hotel staff to come up and join us." He prayed she didn't take him up on that offer, he could just imagine the gossip that would ensue if he had to apologize for the threatened spanking in front of a third party. What a bloody mess.

"You wouldn't mind someone else sitting in?"

What could he say? He'd made the offer and if she chose to take him up on it, he couldn't turn around now and refuse. Shit.

"Mmm...No, sweetheart, I wouldn't mind. I want you to feel comfortable, to feel safe." He swallowed the bile in his throat. The thought of another media scandal made him feel sick. No matter what it cost, he couldn't walk away leaving her feeling as she did now.

"Okay."

"Okay? Okay, as in you're going to call someone and then open the door?"

The click as the door lock released sounded loud as he waited for her answer. She cautiously opened the door to peer at him. Her eyes were like liquid pools, their blue color intensified by her unshed tears. For a brief moment, he couldn't meet her eyes. He was a worthless bastard who didn't deserve a second chance.

He tried to make his smile as reassuring as possible. He had gotten this far, now if she would open the door and let him in he would be able to talk to her properly, settle her fears. Not wanting to crowd her or make her feel threatened; he made no move toward the door.

"I'm sorry, Angel," he said, meaning it. "I was only joking about the spanking." He felt only a twinge of guilt at the lie. "I would never intentionally hurt you; I thought you would have realized that after last night." In truth, he would like nothing more than to spank her, but never without her consent and not with the intent to cause serious pain.

She wouldn't look at him, instead her gaze seemed to be focused somewhere in the middle of his chest as she listened to his apology. Her hands gripped the edge of the door as though ready to slam the door shut at the slightest hint of a threat. Her body was hidden almost totally behind the door.

"My name's Chloe, as you know only too well." She didn't sound in the least forgiving.

"Chloe." He nodded his head acknowledging her, "Are you going to let me in? Or perhaps," he continued, "you would feel better coming back down to the conference suite. I don't care where we do it, but we do need to talk."

"What's left to talk about?" She sounded resigned. "You're hardly likely to give me the position now." She sounded utterly defeated, and he hated it.

"How do you know I won't give you the position? I've not had the chance to interview you yet." He kept his tone light.

"You mean after…" she stuttered nervously. "After last night and this morning, you would still be willing to consider me for the position?" He watched as she flushed in obvious embarrassment.

"I am still considering you for the position," he told her firmly, "but I cannot interview you through a wooden door."

For a second or two, hope flashed across her face. Unwittingly she had given him an advantage. As an executive, he understood the need to know your opponents strengths and weaknesses. If getting the position meant so much to her, and would get him through the door, he certainly wasn't about to let the advantage go. Adrenalin kicked in filling him with confidence. It was time he took charge of the situation if they were going to get past this hiccup in their relationship.

"Come on, Chloe, I don't bite," he coaxed. "You came for an interview so let's get started. Forget this morning, we're both adults and can put it behind us."

Liar. Chloe didn't think she would ever be able to forget how he had made her feel.

She was undecided. She really needed the position and the accommodation, which accompanied it. Could she really trust him? He'd said he was joking about the spanking, but it wasn't the kind of thing people joked about on such short acquaintance, and besides, he hadn't seemed like he was joking. Could she trust him not to use his physical strength against her at some point in the future?

Her thoughts were racing. "I'm not sure. I need to think."

"Take all the time you need, sweetheart."

Xander leaned casually against the doorjamb, looking a lot more relaxed than she felt. He was obviously happy to give her the time to sort out her thoughts.

She tried to get her chaotic thoughts in order, but it was very hard to concentrate with him so close. She did need the position desperately, but if she didn't agree to the interview, she was going to have no chance. However, if she was successful and given the opportunity to work with Xander was she going to be able to put aside this attraction? The position was live-in. How was she going to be able to resist him, to forget what a magnificent lover he was?

What choice did she have? Nick was going to be free in a few weeks and she had to relocate. There had been very few positions she could apply for that offered accommodation, and if she didn't take the chance now being offered she was going to leave herself in easy reach of Nick.

She had debated with herself long enough and he had been very patient. Slowly she nodded her head, agreeing wordlessly to his demands as she opened the door and stepped back to let him enter her suite.

In a few strides, he was in the centre of the small lounge where he stopped and turned around to study her. He was totally still, as if he was holding his breath just waiting to see what she would do. As she approached the sitting area, he smiled gently.

He breathed softly before lowering himself into a chair. He indicated that she should take the chair opposite and she nervously sat down to face him.

"Good girl," he murmured.

Inside she was shaking. She had counted on gaining this position in order to make her escape from Nick, and even though Xander said he still wanted to continue with the interview she couldn't let herself believe that he was sincere. She didn't truly believe she had any chance of securing the post. Her head fell forward in defeat and she couldn't bring herself to look at him. What the hell was she going to do now? Without this position, she would very soon be homeless. She didn't have the funds to leave the area and, with Nick free, she was going to be at risk. It looked like the only choice left would be to contact her stepfather for help, something she was loath to do.

"Eyes on me, Chloe!" His tone brooked no argument.

She lifted her gaze to stare defiantly at him, as she recalled exactly where he had been and what he'd been doing the last time he'd issued that command. By the quirk of his lips, she knew he was also remembering and that thought alone was enough to make her squirm.

"Why do you want this position Chloe?" His eyes never left hers. "Why would someone as young, beautiful and intelligent as you obviously are, want to work somewhere so isolated?"

It wasn't the kind of question she had been expecting. What could she say?

She felt the shame associated with the court case and still struggled to understand why she had put up with Nick's abuse for so long. Why hadn't she walked out earlier? Why hadn't she pressed charges after the first assault? When had she turned into such a coward?

She needed to come up with a convincing lie. There was no way she wanted to explain her previous behavior to him. Her mouth was dry with nerves and she licked her lips nervously as she prepared her reply.

"Well, I'm ready for a change and fed up with the rat race. I thought a change of scenery would do me good and," she added firmly, "I'm well qualified for the position advertised."

For a moment or two, he said nothing. He didn't look happy with her answer, and his face had become a grim mask. She watched as he loosened his tie and rubbed a hand around the back of his neck as if trying to ease his tension. He straightened and looked her straight in the eye, his gaze probing, before he said softly, "Tell me about Nick."

She was caught completely off guard. Of all the questions she could have expected at an interview, that wasn't one of them. She felt light headed with shock. Oh hell! How did he know about Nick?

"How…," she stuttered, "how do you know about Nick?" Fear crawled up her spine; surely, he wasn't involved with Nick.

"I'm a wealthy man, Chloe," he replied tersely. "I make it a point to investigate potential employees before I take them on. Especially," he emphasized, "if that employee is going to be working closely with me." He pulled a large buff envelope from his jacket pocket and handed it to her.

Apprehensively she accepted the envelope, noting the name of a private investigator on the front. She slowly opened the envelope to retrieve the report. He had gotten his money's worth; the report left nothing out. It detailed everything from the death of her mother, the whereabouts of her stepfather, her past affairs and the full transcript from the court case. It contained copies of her college and medical records, noted the state of her perilous bank balance and the fact that the property owner had served notice on her.

She felt raw and exposed. He knew her every secret, had left her with nothing, not even her pride. She shook with rage that he had dared to snoop into her personal life. She felt the blush that blazed across her cheeks as she recalled her 'no names' game of the previous night. Had he been laughing at her? Had he already known all her secrets then? Had it amused him to know who she really was when she didn't have a clue about him?

The interview was turning into a farce. In despair, she searched his face. How could she trust him now?

"Now you know what I know. Shall we start again?" Xander's tone brooked no argument. "And don't ever lie to me again, Chloe!" He said firmly, his jaw tense.

She didn't know where to start. This interview had turned into a nightmare. She could feel the panic welling up in her chest and suddenly she was struggling to breathe. She was about to go into full melt down and could feel tears of mortification welling in her eyes. She had to get away. She shot to her feet and bolted for the door, not caring that she'd dropped the file and scattered its contents all over the floor.

For a big man Xander moved quickly. He was at her back his hand pressed against the door to prevent her opening it before she realized he had even moved. Panic clawed at her chest as she tried desperately to open the door, to escape. Her strength was no match for his opposing force.

She slumped forward resting her head against the door. She was defeated. Xander was at her back, his hands resting on the door above her head, caging her with his body and effectively preventing her escape. All her efforts to stay strong over the last few months dissolved in a puddle of tears she was helpless to prevent. She sank to the floor and buried her face in her hands as she sobbed out her desolation.

She was startled when she felt his firm grip on her shoulder. Not asking for permission, he turned her, picked her up and strode back to sit in his chair with her cradled in his lap. She should insist he put her down, maybe tell him to leave but she couldn't. He was holding her firmly, his confining arms rocking her gently and, for the first time in a long while, she felt safe.

For a long time he said nothing, just held her close as he stroked his fingers in light circles over her back. He left her to cry herself out against his chest until her sobs became no more than light hiccups and the front of his shirt was soaked with her tears. With her crying bout over, she once again considered asking him to leave. She made an effort to pull herself together, but as she tried to raise herself away from his chest and off his lap, he held her firm.

"Stay still." He placed a firm finger under her chin and lifted her face up so she had to look at him. He dabbed at her face with his handkerchief, blotting away her tears. He looked so concerned and, for a little while, she allowed herself to bask in being taken care of. She had felt alone for such a long time and it was lovely to have someone show her warmth and compassion.

"Okay, now that's over," he sat her up on his lap but did not release her. "Tell me what the hell that was all about." He did not raise his voice, but his tone was firm. She swallowed nervously. He really did deserve an explanation.

He kept eye contact, never once looking away from her. It was slightly unnerving as though he could read every thought she had ever had. Chloe shivered in his arms and his grip tightened.

She didn't know where to start. How did she explain to a prospective employer, who also happened to be a gorgeous sexy man, how much of a fool she had been in the past? How did she explain that she really was responsible and capable of holding down a job, when she had made such a mess of her own life? How did she explain how weak she had been? Dumbfounded, she could only stare at him.

"Chloe, I'm waiting." His tone was clipped.

She couldn't tell him what she had been through and look him in the eye at the same time; it was just too embarrassing. She turned her gaze away from him and looked over his shoulder at the skyline beyond the window. Slowly she recounted her relationship with Nick, the assault and the subsequent court case. How she had been unable to work due to her injuries and how she feared Nick being released from prison.

She could feel Xander tense beneath her and when she recanted her injuries, his breath hissed between his teeth. She cast him a quick glance and could see his jaw was tense and his eyes looked like coal chips, dark and dangerous; no longer the deep hazel that she had drowned in the previous night. He pulled her closer, holding her enfolded against his chest. She didn't want his pity but she couldn't help but feel safer than she had in a long time as she cuddled up against him. For a moment or two, she allowed herself the luxury of pretending that this was where she belonged.

For a little while, they sat in silence. She was exhausted and had nothing else to add to her story.

"So, Chloe…," he stated hoarsely, "you really need this position in order to relocate; not be where Nick can find you upon his release?"

She nodded slowly in reply.

"Yes," she whispered, hardly able to believe that he seemed about to offer her the position. She added, "I am qualified as a PA and I'm good at my job. I work hard and would earn my salary, I'm not asking for charity."

She couldn't believe after all that had transpired in the last twenty four hours, that he was still considering her for the post. Hope rose once again as she awaited his answer

"Okay." Xander lifted her effortlessly from his lap and sat her on the coffee table in front of him.

He pulled his chair towards the table and positioned himself so that she was sat between his legs, his hands resting on her thighs he looked up into her face.

"I need to think this over." He continued to caress her thighs making small circular swirls with his thumbs, which robbed her of her concentration. "I want you to have a rest while I nip into the office. I will be back to see you this afternoon."

"But I'm supposed to check out at noon!" she said. She was disappointed. Was he using business as an excuse to prevent telling her face to face that he was not going to give her the position?

"I'll sort the hotel, don't worry about it." He waved his hand as though he could arrange anything. "Now, be a good girl and take a rest while you wait for me." He smiled broadly, "I know you didn't get much sleep last night."

He was back to being Mr. Dominant and she wasn't sure she liked it; there was no trace of softness in his face now, his features were hard and determined.

"Does this mean I've got the job?" she asked tremulously. She needed an answer. She would never be able to relax enough to take a nap with her future so uncertain.

"We'll discuss it later, Chloe." His tone brooked no argument.

He stood abruptly as though he was in a rush to get away. He planted a short firm kiss on her lips before he turned and strode to the door.

"Have a nap." He held up his hand to forestall her objection. "No excuses. You're exhausted."

He looked at his watch and, just like that, she knew she was being dismissed. She huffed and puffed a bit, pretending indignation at his high handedness but was secretly thrilled when his eyes shot warning sparks at her. What was it about him that made her want to obey? She had resented Nick's controlling ways, but Xander showing his dominance didn't get her back up the same way. It did however make her feel flustered in a completely different, entirely pleasurable way.

She was sure now that he was going to offer her the position, after all why would he pay to extend her hotel stay if he were not going to employ her? Why would he be coming back to see her if not to discuss terms and the position he wanted filled?

She cursed herself for not asking him for more details about the role; hadn't the advert stated the position was to work for a craftsman? Xander looked more like a business tycoon than any craftsman she had ever seen. It was only later as she sat waiting for him to return that she started to question what he really did. She wished she had brought her laptop so that she could Google him, but she hadn't so she was just going to have to wait and get the answers from Xander himself.

Chapter Four

She didn't feel tired enough to take a nap, but decided instead to relax for a while with the book she had started the previous evening. She didn't know how long it would be before he returned but guessed that she would have at least an hour or two to herself as he expected her to be sleeping.

After a scant half hour, she gave up on her book. How could she be expected to relax when she didn't know what her future was going to hold? As she paced her hotel room, weighing her chances of getting the position, she caught sight of her reflection in the mirror. Good Lord, she looked a fright. Her eyes were still red from her crying bout and her makeup had just about disappeared.

She decided to have a quick shower. She quickly stripped out of her clothes, stepped into the cubicle and scrubbed herself under the warm water. The heat helped to ease her aching muscles and made her aware of how tense she had been. She would have liked to linger a while but she didn't want Xander catch her undressed and at a disadvantage. She had just finished toweling herself dry when she heard his sharp rap on the door. In a panic, she scrabbled around trying to pull on clean underwear. She hollered for him to wait.

He knocked again, obviously not a patient man. Having gotten into her underwear, she pulled the hotel's terry toweling robe from the back of the bathroom door, fastening the belt securely around her middle, as she went to let him in.

"About time," he snapped as he strode purposefully into the room.

It was just the kind of thing Nick would have said and she resented it. Was he expecting her to be standing ready to let him in when he had given no indication of his expected arrival time? It was time she stood up for herself. She refused to be treated like a doormat again.

"I was trying to get dressed," she snapped. "I didn't expect you so soon."

She closed the door and turned to face him. He stood in the middle of the room, legs splayed, arms crossed, as he surveyed her from head to foot. She could see the heat of desire in his eyes as he studied her. Her flesh tingled and heat pooled between her legs. She felt like he had caressed her with his hands and not just his eyes. She squirmed, as he smiled at her discomfort. She was sure that he was aware of her arousal.

"Go and get dressed Chloe," he said. "Then we'll talk."

"But--" She had wanted to ask him to leave, to give her time to get dressed before they talked. She didn't feel comfortable with him sitting in the suite waiting for her to dress. It felt altogether too intimate.

"No 'buts', unless you want to do something other than talk." He watched her with narrowed eyes then he uncrossed his arms and walked slowly towards her, a mischievous grin on his face.

She turned away, quickly heading for the bathroom.

"Take a seat. I won't be long." She threw the words over her shoulder, catching the surprised expression on his face. The man was just too much of a distraction. She should be concentrating on securing a position which would help her relocate, not drooling over her prospective employer.

She dressed quickly in the blouse and trousers she had already laid out in the bathroom, applied a light coating of makeup and secured her hair in a neat French twist. Looking in the mirror she was pleased to see that once again she looked presentable for an interview.

She returned to the small lounge area a scant ten minutes later, to find that Xander had made himself at home. He was lounging on the small sofa, the ankle of one leg resting across the knee of the other, nursing a drink from her mini bar.

He gestured to the small coffee table where a glass of wine sat waiting for her.

"I took the liberty of pouring you a drink."

"Thanks." She looked at her watch and saw it was only just gone noon. "But it's a bit early for me. I'm not much of a drinker."

"I'll have a soft drink." She reached into the mini bar and withdrew a can of cola.

Nervous, not at all sure of where this meeting was leading, she took a seat in a chair on the opposite side of the coffee table.

At first he said nothing, just sat looking at her. He seemed totally at ease and her nervousness increased. Was he going to offer her the job or was he just playing with her?

"Mr. Doumas--"

"It's a bit late to go formal," he cut in, with a wicked grin and a wink, "Xander will do."

"Well then, Xander," she rushed, "are you going to offer me the position I applied for?"

"I'm not sure," he replied earnestly. "I don't like to mix business with pleasure." He looked her straight in the eye.

Her stomach sank, the one and only one-night stand in her life had backfired on her spectacularly. She opened her mouth to protest. It wasn't fair that he had given her false hope, but he held up his hand to stall her. "However, I do want to help you," he continued, "and I don't want you anywhere near Nick."

She was perplexed. If he wasn't going to offer her the job, what was he offering? She raised her eyebrow in enquiry, waiting to hear what he had to say.

He suddenly dropped his crossed leg to the floor, and sat forward on the couch. Legs splayed, forearms resting on his muscular thighs, he cradled the drink in his hand as he leaned towards her across the table.

"My dilemma," he said, "is that I need a PA and quite honestly you were the only candidate even worth considering. Out of the other two that I interviewed one was old enough to be my grandmother and the other, well let's just say that she recognized me and it wasn't the job she was after." His features were grim, and he didn't look at her.

He shrugged his shoulders and she got the feeling he was embarrassed. But why? What was it about him that caused women to try to get close to him? She cursed herself for not having had the foresight to investigate him and his company a little before attending the interview.

Her brain had stopped functioning at the part where he said she was the only candidate worth considering.

"Great. You're going to offer me the job then," she stated.

"No."

No! Her stomach sank. She was running out of options and had pinned all her hopes on getting this job. What was she going to do now? "No," she replied puzzled, "I thought you said I was the only suitable candidate?"

"That's the problem."

"It doesn't feel like a problem to me." She didn't understand.

"Well, it is a problem, because I want to offer you an entirely different position," he replied.

"What position?"

"How does mistress sound?" He looked her straight in the eye, never blinking, as he awaited her reaction.

Shock held her rigid. She must have misheard him, but one look at his face and she knew she had heard him correctly. "You are joking?" She stared at him aghast.

"No, I'm not." He twirled his glass before downing the remaining contents in one gulp. "I need a PA," he continued, "but, I want you in my bed a damn sight more than I need admin help." His tone was clipped and he slapped his glass down on the coffee table with a resounding thud.

Desire coursed through her, and she could feel herself responding to him. Moisture pooled at the juncture of her thighs and her nipples tingled, pushing against her lace bra. The thought of making love to him again was delicious but it still didn't solve her financial problems or her need to relocate. She needed to keep her wits about her and stay sensible.

"And how's that going to help me?" She asked softly. "I need to get a job, Xander; I need to be able to relocate where Nick can't find me."

"As my mistress you wouldn't need a job," he replied arrogantly. "You would be staying with me so no need to look for another place yourself."

She gave him ten out of ten for sheer nerve. What made him think she would ever agree to be his mistress? She could feel her anger rising, her chest felt tight and she struggled to control her breathing. She bit her lip in an effort to stem the tears she could feel threatening.

"Oh yes, it's as easy as that." She snapped her fingers in the air. "How the hell am I going to support myself, pay my bills, and store my stuff?" Had the last couple of days just been a waste of time? Time she didn't have.

Agitated she rose from her chair and walked across the room to stand and stare out of the window. She wanted to look anywhere other than at him. She didn't want him to see how insulted she felt by his offer. Maybe he was a good catch, and perhaps other women queued up to be his bed partner. She couldn't help but feel that if their night together hadn't happened he would never have made her such an offer. Did he think she was cheap?

The view across the Thames would normally have enchanted her, but she was too disappointed at the turn of events to pay it much attention. She swung around to confront Xander and found herself almost cheek to cheek with him. He had come up behind her so quietly she had been unaware that he was there. He was so close she had to retreat a step and tilt her head back to look him in the eye.

"Why?" She looked directly at him. "Why would you want me as your mistress? You're not unattractive; you're obviously reasonably well off. Why the hell would you have to pay someone to be with you?" She shook her head in confusion.

"I don't need to pay someone to be with me!" He replied sharply.

"Then why?"

"Why?" He mused. "Because I want you and because I want to help you." He continued before she could ask any more questions, "Because I want control. I want to know that this time we're playing the game by my rules."

She was perplexed. What did he mean 'playing by his rules'? "I don't understand."

He reached out to take her hand, tugging her gently toward the couch.

"I know. That's part of the problem." He spoke softly as he pulled her down beside him.

"Look, just hear me out. I'll explain what I want and why, if after you have listened to everything I have to say you want to turn me down, then I'll abide by your decision." He watched her intently, and she felt like she was being examined under a microscope. What was he looking for? She wished she could control her trembling limbs and, in an effort to hide her nervousness, she clasped her hands tightly together. "There's no need to be afraid of me, Chloe, I would never hurt you. The final decision is always yours. You are in control."

She got the feeling he was talking about something other than the job or his offer to make her his mistress. His offer had thrown her thoughts into chaos and she couldn't think straight. She had run out of options but, surely, she hadn't sunk so low that she would allow him to buy her had she?

Frantically she tried to think of an alternative. There had to be another way out of her dilemma, but she couldn't think of a single one.

"Okay," she nodded. "I'll hear you out."

He started off slowly, telling her about his businesses, his wealth. When he explained that he was never sure if a woman was with him because of who he was and what he had, or with him purely because she wanted to be, he looked lost. Surely, he couldn't be serious? The man was an idiot! Any woman would want to be with him, did he not realize how gorgeous he was? He was a natural babe magnet and sexy as hell.

He told her of his last disastrous relationship, how he felt he had lost control, how the media frenzy had annoyed him, wreaked havoc on his life and his sister's life. His face was grim as he explained that he did not want to go through something like that again. His solution therefore was to take a mistress on his terms. He wanted a mistress, one who would be happy to sign a confidentiality agreement to keep what went on in their relationship secret, to never 'kiss and tell' to the gossip rags. As his mistress, she would be well provided for, he named a monthly allowance that nearly caused her to pass out it was so much. He promised that he would keep her safe, that his wealth would ensure her safety and her security; she would never have to worry about Nick again. The thought of the security alone was enough to tempt her to consider his proposition.

Xander finished talking and sat quietly watching her. She wouldn't look at him. Inside his guts were churning. He knew he was being a bastard offering to help only on his terms but he wanted more of her; he wanted to have access to her body and her mind. He wanted to explore her possible submissive tendencies. He hoped she would agree to his proposition. But if she turned him down, he would still help her escape Nick's grasp. There was no way he would let the arsehole get his hands on her again.

Finally, she looked at him and said, "If I agree to become your mistress, how are you going to get your admin work done?"

It was the last thing he had expected her to be thinking about. Why the hell was she thinking about admin work when he had just offered her a far better position as his mistress?

"Who gives a damn about the admin work?" He ground out.

"Well, you did, obviously, or you would never have advertised for help in the first place," she replied.

"Are you telling me you would rather have the job as my PA than become my mistress?" He couldn't believe it; women were always trying to get his attention. He was known for his generosity to his lovers, and yet here she was about to turn him down.

"N-n-no…" she stuttered, "I'm just saying that I can't see why I can't do the job and be your girlfriend at the same time."

Had she not heard a word he'd said? Why the hell did women have to complicate things?

"I don't want a girlfriend, Chloe," he replied, "I want a mistress who will abide by my rules."

"Well, I don't like the idea of being paid to sleep with you and—"

"You are not being paid to sleep with me," he cut in sternly. "Do you want to sleep with me, Chloe? Do you want me to take you back to bed and make you scream for release?"

He cursed himself for being an arrogant bastard! He could see the blush that warmed her from her head to foot. She didn't have to answer, he knew she wanted him, but she wasn't going to admit it to him. He only had to look at her to see the glazed look that came over her face when she recalled their previous encounter, and he knew he had her. He pushed his advantage.

"Okay, Chloe, you win," he said as if it were a major concession. If letting her think she had won got him what he wanted, namely her in his bed every day, then he was happy to let her think she had won the first battle.

"You're going to give me the job?" She asked uncertainly.

He shook his head. "No, I'm not going to give you the job," he said firmly, feeling like a bastard when disappointment clouded her eyes. "But," he continued quickly, "I am willing to let you help out if it makes you feel better about accepting an allowance; you can tell yourself it's wages. I am not putting you on the payroll. If you come with me, you come with me as my mistress."

She sank back against the deep cushions of the couch as if trying to distance herself from him. Her teeth nibbled away at her bottom lip and she eyed him warily as she clasped her hands tightly in her lap. Was she going to turn him down? He'd expected her to be happy about his offer. He certainly hadn't thought he'd have to work so hard to talk her into accepting it. He watched as she struggled to stifle a yawn. He noted the dark smudges under her eyes and felt guilty. It was his fault she was sleep deprived.

"How long do I get to decide?" She watched him through half closed eyes, and he could see exhaustion catching up with her.

"You have until tomorrow morning, Chloe," he told her, "at which time I have to return home."

"I need time to think. I can't make a decision like that overnight."

"I can't give you any longer." His tone was even but uncompromising.

He was being unfair asking her to make a life changing decision in a few hours, but he refused to back down and lose his advantage. He was sure that once she had a chance to rest she would see reason and the logic in his solution. He softened his tone as he continued, "Chloe, go and have a nap, see how you feel about things when you are rested." He handed her his business card, "Give me a call when you wake up and I'll take you out to dinner."

"How the hell do you expect me to sleep when I've got so much to think about?" She frowned mutinously.

He wasn't used to being questioned or talked back to in that manner by anyone; most people 'bowed and scraped' their way around him, and none of his previous girlfriends would have questioned his authority. He had to remind himself that, as yet, she wasn't his submissive. He'd spotted her potential and wanted to explore it further, but she had no idea about his hopes for their future. He needed more time with her to build up the necessary trust between them before he broached the subject.

He sighed, not used to having to tread warily with women. He leaned back with his arms crossed as he looked at her. "Chloe, you are shattered. Get your backside off the couch and go and take a nap," he said softly. "Or do you want me to undress you myself and put you into bed?"

Her eyes widened as she looked at him. She licked her lips and he could see she was wondering if he would carry through on his threat.

Did he dare? She'd run from him when he had threatened to spank her and he didn't want to frighten her. He thought about it for a moment or two and decided she had to know that he meant what he said. If she was going to be his mistress, she had to learn to follow his instructions without question. She knew now that he wanted control in their relationship so his actions shouldn't come as too much of a surprise. Without pausing to consider further he stood and scooped her up in his arms. She gave a surprised shriek as he carried her into the bedroom.

He put her down just in front of the bed, and ignoring her murmured protests, set about efficiently stripping off her clothes. Ineffectively, she tried to stall his progress.

"Xander, for goodness sake. Stop!"

"No way, sweetheart. You're tired and if you won't get yourself into bed, then I will put you there." His tone was grim. "You've got to learn to trust me, to know that I only want what is best for you."

He had her down to her underwear in no time. Modestly she tried to cover herself with her arms, an action he found endearing considering he had already tasted all of her. He pulled back the bedcover, picked her up and set her unceremoniously in the middle of the bed. He undid her front fastening bra and removed it before running his fingers slowly between her breasts, over her stomach to the patch of lace covering her sex. All the time she just lay there, watching him. She slowly licked at her lips as she followed the line of his fingers. Her nipples peaked and she trembled slightly beneath his hand. God, he loved how responsive she was.

He was so tempted to join her, to taste every inch of her before he sheathed himself inside her welcoming body. He uttered a low groan as his carnal thoughts caused blood to flow south. He was already achingly hard. If he didn't get himself out of there quickly he was going to end up joining her in the bed and she would get no rest. Without ceremony, he pulled the scrap of lace down her legs and tossed it over his shoulder. He pulled the covers over her, hiding her tempting body from view, and tucked her in like a child.

"Now get some sleep, baby girl." He traced the dark smudges under her eyes gently, "You're worn out. I'll be back later for your decision."

Chloe wriggled restlessly under the covers. She didn't look pleased that he was leaving and she positively pouted as she complained, "How do you expect me to sleep when I've so much to think about? My mind is churning."

His patience and resolve snapped. "Well, I can soon sort that!" he ground out as he collapsed onto the bed at her side, "I know just the thing to relax you."

Chloe was exultant when he took possession of her mouth. He drove her mad with his high-handed attitude yet she couldn't help but glory in the feel of his lips on hers. His tongue traced the seam of her lips as his hand held her jaw firm, not allowing her to move away from him. On a sigh, her lips parted allowing his tongue access to plunder at will. That she could break his resolve left her feeling powerful. She wasn't the only one enthralled by the chemistry between them, their attraction was obviously mutual.

Good Lord, the man could kiss. So far, he had done nothing but kiss her. Her insides were melting and she could feel the heat building at the juncture of her thighs. Unable to help herself, she whimpered in need. She needed more; she needed him. Trying to get closer she wriggled her hips invitingly against him and was rewarded when he ground his thigh against her mound, causing a delicious friction which only served to send her need spiraling higher.

He let go of her jaw as he entwined his fingers around her wrists, lifting her arms above her head and placing her hands around the bars on the bed head.

"Keep them there, sweetheart." He told her firmly as he dragged the cover away.

She watched his eyes darken as they traveled the length of her body. He took his time surveying her as his heated gaze traveled from head to foot. Suddenly it felt like his hands were everywhere. He molded her breasts in the palms of his hands before bending his head to nip sharply on her nipples, taking each in turn to give each the bruising treatment before gently laving each with his tongue. She couldn't help but give a small cry at the short sharp pain and didn't understand why this would make her sex spasm and clench in need. His hands traveled down over her stomach to the apex of her thighs. He pushed against a thigh firmly, opening her to his touch and her hips rose off the bed in anticipation. When his fingers stroked along her slit, sliding in quick flicks to the side of her clit, but not quite hitting the spot she wriggled trying to position herself nearer his fingers.

He chuckled and raised his head to smile at her. "I can see my baby girl is getting impatient," he winked, "I'll soon have you sorted, darling."

Oh good Lord, the heat in his eyes was enough to melt snow and she relaxed back into the mattress on a whimper; she was in so much trouble. She reached out for him needing to pull him closer.

"Assume the position." Suddenly he wasn't smiling any more.

"What?" She was confused and disappointed. What did he mean 'assume the position'? Why wasn't she allowed to touch him?

He grabbed her wrists and returned her hands to the headboard, "I told you, I like control. Keep your hands there." His tone brooked no argument. "Don't move them again."

She gripped the bedstead tightly, anything as long as he would continue with what he was doing before.

"Hold on tight, baby girl," he smiled at her "you're about to get your reward!"

Oh shit. Once more, his hands dived between her legs, opening her up fully to his view. She felt the heat of her blush and watched as his gaze followed the tide of heat that rose on her skin. His eyes blazed as he dipped his head between her legs and slowly curled his tongue around her clit. He stroked the tip back and forth across her most sensitive bud, causing moisture to pool and intense clenching to start below.

Lost in sensation her hips undulated to the sweep of his tongue, trying to get closer, reaching out for her release. He continued to lap and suck as he stroked his fingers into her, bringing her closer and closer to the edge.

She was getting close to release, her thighs trembled and her pussy walls were gripping his fingers tighter and tighter. He raised his head to look at her and she watched him smile with pleasure when he noted her hands held firm where he had positioned them. Unable to help herself her body arched off the bed with need.

"Eyes on me, baby girl," he groaned, "remember my rules."

Xander watched as she lifted her head from the pillow to stare into his eyes. Whether or not she could focus on him he didn't really know or care, he just needed to see her reaction when he finally took her over the edge. He pulled himself up the bed to lie at her side. Propped on one elbow he stared down at her as he stroked her vigorously. He slid his fingers through her moist heat from the top of her slit, across her clit, and down to her channel where he dipped his fingers inside her to stroke her G-spot. As his fingers stroked internally he kept his thumb moving, constantly caressing her clit.

"Oh God…" she whimpered. "Please, please…"

Shit, he loved the way she begged for her release. "Please what, baby girl?"

"Xander, please…" She was so near and he loved that he could bring her to the height of passion so quickly. She really was very responsive. She looked at him, pleading with her eyes for him to do something, anything to end the torment and give her the release her body was seeking.

He dipped his head and wrapped his lips around a nipple, pulling and sucking forcefully; his fingers could feel the reaction of her body as her internal muscles clenched tightly around him. Stroking his fingers in and out of her moist channel, he spread the moisture front to back, ensuring he caught her now erect clit on each stroke; he wanted her as close to the edge as he could get her without taking her over until he was ready.

He lifted his head to look at her, her eyes met his and he made his decision. May as well give her a taste of what he liked if she was going to agree to become his mistress. Lowering his head to capture her mouth his lips forced her head into the pillow as he took his index finger, now fully lubricated with her own juices, and slid it into her backside.

As he entered her behind, she went rigid, her eyes locking on to his with shock. Obviously, no one had ever tried that with her before. He liked the thought that he was the first. Not releasing her mouth, he continued to stroke his tongue in and out, mimicking his fingers as they rocked in and out of her. He slowly twirled the finger inserted into her backside, pulling and pushing as he opened up her virgin hole. All the time he watched her. He knew the moment when she finally gave in to the new sensation. He felt the shudder that trembled over her from head to foot when she finally relaxed into his hold and let her body have its own way.

Releasing her mouth, he coaxed her to the end. "I can see you like that." He whispered, hoarsely, "I am so looking forward to burying my cock in your ass, sweetheart. You are going to feel so tight, so full. Soon, baby. Soon."

He didn't know if it was his words, the images they conjured up or the fact that he was still stroking her, but suddenly she was there, she had climbed the peak. "Yes! Yes! Yes!" She screamed as her orgasm hit and she shook from head to toe as her climax rolled through her, before tossing her back onto the bed like a limp rag doll.

God, he loved watching her cum! He held her close as her climax subsided and watched in amazement as she almost immediately fell asleep. He fetched a washcloth and towel from the bathroom and gently washed between her legs; he didn't want her to wake up sore later. He covered her nakedness with the bedding, hiding temptation. He was still fully dressed and had done no more than kick off his shoes as he assuaged her hunger. He allowed himself a short while to hold her close, or as close as he could get with her bundled up in the covers. She needed to rest and he was sure she would sleep now that he had helped her to relax.

He was about to leave, when Chloe opened her eyes to look at him.

"Xander, I'm so sorry."

"What are you sorry for, sweetheart?" He was puzzled. Was she going to turn down his offer after all?

She indicated his clothing. "What about you? Christ, I never even let you get undressed." She didn't meet his eyes as she spoke.

"Don't worry about me, darling," he laughed, relieved. "I had just about as much fun watching you."

"I've been so selfish, I'm so embarrassed."

He gripped her jaw firmly, forcing her to look at him. "There's no need to be embarrassed Chloe. Not now, not ever, with me," he told her gently. "I love watching you cum. I get as much pleasure, seeing your pleasure, as you do succumbing to me. Christ, I could watch you cum all day!"

"Now," he tucked the covers firmly around her, "get some sleep. I've got things to see to this afternoon, but I will be back to pick you up for dinner."

Chapter Five

Chloe awoke refreshed and rested as the afternoon was coming to a close. Looking at the bedside table she saw on the clock that it was nearly six o'clock; she had slept the whole afternoon away.

Xander was coming back to take her out to dinner which meant she had better move herself and get ready though, for the life of her, she didn't know what she was going to wear. Having planned on being in town for only the one night to attend her interview, she had very few clothes with her. She resigned herself to the fact that she would probably just have to re-wear the palazzo pants she had worn the previous evening.

She showered in the en suite and emerged wrapped once again in the hotel bathrobe. She wandered into the bedroom intent on drying her hair and applying some makeup before Xander reappeared.

A knock at the door caused her to curse under her breath. Christ, the man hadn't given her enough time to get dressed. She crossed the room briskly, intent on sending him away for a while until she was ready. However, it was not Xander at the door as she had expected. Instead, to her surprise, a porter swept into the room, his arms bulging with parcels. He gave a sigh of relief as he cautiously unloaded himself and placed the parcels on the coffee table.

"With the compliments of Mr. Doumas, Madame," he said, rather pompously.

Chloe was flustered at being caught in a state of undress, and she fumbled in her handbag, looking for her wallet to tip the man.

"No need, Madame," he backed courteously away from her, "Mr. Doumas has already taken care of everything."

She closed the door behind the porter then turned to view the pile of boxes, all bearing exclusive designer labels, which now sat in the middle of the room. She spied a card attached to the top box and crossed to snatch the envelope up. Her eyes widened as she read his note, written in bold black strokes. 'Wear the black dress tonight. It will do wonders for you!'

Arrogant bastard! Who the hell did he think he was? She'd had enough of men telling her what to wear; she wasn't about to go down that path again. Stubbornly she refused to open the boxes. He could stuff his clothes and his orders. She was going to wear what she wanted to wear, not what he instructed her to wear. Never again was she going to be dictated to.

She returned to the bedroom to dry her hair and dress in her original choice of pants and loose cotton top, before applying a light coating of makeup.

Unsure as to what time Xander would be calling to collect her; she sat in the lounge enjoying a small glass of white wine from the mini bar. She would have to talk to him about the shocking proposition he had made earlier in the day. At this point in her life, she needed a job and an income. She did not need another man who wanted to control her.

It was obvious he lived in a completely different world from her, a wealthy world where he could have anything he wanted. She had to watch every penny she spent, he could afford to throw money around as if it wasn't important. She looked at the parcels still unopened on the table. The labels alone proclaimed they were well out of her reach. She didn't even want to think about how much money he must have spent.

Money wasn't their only difference. Having a mistress may be normal in his world, but not in hers. Sure, she'd had lovers in the past, but they were normal relationships. She had believed herself in love with her partner. Okay, things hadn't always worked out the way she had hoped and, to be honest, living with Nick had turned into a living nightmare. Xander's proposition, on the other hand, seemed so calculated, so cold. He had said he didn't want a girlfriend. So, what did he want? He'd talked about control. But she had zero interest in giving her control to a man again.

However, she could not discount the fact that the feelings he evoked in her were anything but cold. He was the sexiest man she had ever come across. The fact that he professed his need for her was such a turn on. The man was dynamite!

As she sat, pondering on what she was going to say to him, the telephone rang.

"Hello," she answered the telephone tentatively, "Chloe here."

Without preamble, his deep voice came back in reply. "I've been held up in a meeting, so a car will be coming to pick you up in thirty minutes. Are you wearing the black dress?" His voice was expectant.

"No, I'm not," she fired back, sharper than she had intended; "I'm wearing my own clothes!"

He responded with a deep sigh before he told her, "We're having dinner with some clients I've been landed with. I didn't think you would have anything suitable with you, hence my gift." His tone was even and patient, and now she felt churlish.

Shit, shit, shit! She looked down at her outfit; it may be suitable for a casual dinner but no way was it suitable for a business dinner and he was correct, she had nothing suitable with her. Now she was going to be short of time to change. Wasn't it just typical of a man to give you no warning of his plans?

"Christ, you could give a girl more warning!"

"Well, it wasn't exactly what I planned, but they are important clients and I can't get out of it. I'm stuck with entertaining them for the evening."

"Maybe," she offered, trying to hide her disappointment, "you would be better off on your own."

"Oh no, you don't," he replied quickly, "you're not getting out of it that easily. I promised you dinner and dinner it is. I still want to see you."

And, she really needed to see him. She was still hoping to talk to him about his proposition, perhaps if they had dinner and he was in a good mood she could reason with him, persuade him to give her the job. She would just have to put aside her attraction to him.

"Well, get off the phone and let me go and get changed!" She cried into the mouthpiece, clearly flustered.

"Thirty minutes, lady, that's all you've got." He continued firmly, "Wear the black dress. I've been fantasizing about seeing you in it all afternoon."

She was given no chance to reply, as the dial tone sounded on the telephone indicating that he had hung up, without giving her a chance to voice her objections.

First things first, she had to get the boxes through to the bedroom and start to open them; she had to find the black dress. It took three trips just to transport all the packages and she looked at them scattered across the bed, wondering just where to start. Frantically, she tore packages open, oh Good Lord, the man had gone overboard.

She had unwrapped underwear, shoes, cosmetics, and several other dresses before she found the only black dress there. A short lace sheath, lined in silk, which bore a Chanel label, the dress was deceptively demure. The halter neck was cut modestly low at the front, but the back plunged stopping just short of her waist. She would definitely be going bra-less, her only underwear a pair of sensually soft, black silk mini briefs, trimmed with lace, and the sheer hold-up stockings which had accompanied them in the parcel.

Dressed in the complete ensemble she stepped in front of the mirror to admire her reflection. The dress fit like a glove and ended mid-thigh; she swallowed the lump in her throat. It had been so long since she had allowed herself to wear anything overtly sexy for fear of incurring Nick's wrath, that she had forgotten what it felt like to be a desirable woman. Xander obviously didn't see her the same way as Nick; the clothes he had provided were made to enhance her femininity, not hide it. How he had managed to guess her sizes, she didn't know nor at that moment, did she care. If things didn't go according to plan tonight, she may never see him again. She was determined to enjoy what may very well be her last night with him and not worry about little details.

She finished off the outfit with a pair of ridiculously high Louboutin patent heels with their distinctive red soles, also provided by Xander. Breathless from rushing to change, Chloe felt sexier than she had in a long time. On a high, she blew herself a kiss in the mirror. She could feel her excitement start to mount at the thought of seeing Xander again.

Exactly thirty minutes later, just as he had predicted, reception called to inform her that the car had arrived.

Exiting the hotel entrance she had to stifle a giggle when she saw the black limo, complete with tinted windows and a chauffeur waiting for her. Christ, the man didn't do things by half! She was slightly embarrassed as other hotel patrons, coming and going from the hotel, as well as passersby, stopped to stare at her as she entered the rear of the vehicle. She felt like a celebrity and wondered what they would say if she told them she was nothing but a humble secretary on her way out for the evening. Money sure did attract attention.

The car had only just pulled away from the curb and into traffic when her mobile rang. She didn't recognize the number but hit the answer button anyway.

"Are you in the car?" He asked without preamble.

"Hello, Xander," she replied huskily, "What do you think?"

"I think," he growled down the line, "that the quicker you learn to answer my questions, the easier it will be for you. I will make you pay for teasing me." His voice was full of sensual promise, not threat, and she could feel the thrill course through her body at the thought of the ways he would make her pay.

Rested and in a playful mood, she giggled as she replied, "Promises, promises!"

"You're playing with fire, sweetheart." She could hear the smile in his voice and imagine the gleam in his eye. He didn't sound at all cross and she allowed herself to sink back into the leather seat, relaxing as the car wound its way towards him.

"Are you wearing the dress?"

"Yes, and it's lovely. Thank you for--"

"And the silk underwear?" He cut in before she could thank him properly.

She could feel herself blush, she wasn't used to discussing her underwear with her men friends and she remained silent.

"Chloe, I'm not going to ask you again." Xander's tone was impatient, "Answer me."

"Yes," she answered quietly, embarrassed at his question, "I'm also wearing the other things you provided." She cast a furtive glance at the chauffeur hoping he couldn't hear her conversation.

"Why are you whispering?"

"Well…" she turned her head to the side, looking out the window as she whispered indignantly into the phone, "I don't want the chauffeur hearing me discussing my undies!"

His responding laughter was not the response she expected.

"Xander, behave!" She scolded him.

"Are you blushing, baby girl?" He had stopped laughing now and his voice was low, heavy with need.

"No, no….. Hell, yes!" She finally snapped, annoyed with him for making her admit it.

She heard the moan issued deep from the back of his throat, "Have you any idea," he groaned, "what that does to me?"

Even though he couldn't see her, she shook her head in a negative response as she wondered exactly what it was it did to him.

With no response from her, he continued, "I am so hard now, baby girl. I can't wait to bury myself deep inside you; I'm going to be soaked in all your honey when you next cum."

Oh God, she was going to dissolve in a puddle here. "Xander, please…" she needed to stop him talking, "I can't have this conversation with you now." Mortified, she remembered the afternoon when he had assured her pleasure but taken none for himself. She snapped her phone closed, effectively ending the conversation. Her pants were already damp and she could feel her internal muscles tremble; his voice alone turned her on. Oh shit, she was in deep trouble. How the hell could she ever refuse him when he made her feel so good?

On the journey to meet Xander, she had plenty of time to think about his proposal. It seemed unreal that he would want her as his mistress although she could not discount his obvious passionate response to her. In truth, it would solve an awful lot of problems. She would be able to relocate, she would not have to worry about funds, and she would have a new protector in Xander. However, could she trust him? She had no reason to doubt his word and apart from the misunderstanding when he had threatened to spank her, he had given her no reason to fear him. Of course, neither had Nick in the beginning, she reminded herself.

She weighed the pros and cons of his offer; everything seemed to be stacked in her favor if she could just get over her aversion to the title of mistress. She would relish the role of girlfriend or live-in lover, either of which seemed so much more normal. She wondered why the idea of being his mistress upset her.

Maybe, she pondered, it was more of a cultural thing. She had heard that many married men on the Continent had mistresses. It seemed almost expected. Nevertheless, she reminded herself, she wasn't going to be a mistress tucked away in her own little apartment where he would visit discreetly. He had asked her to live with, and travel with, him. Maybe this was his way of compensating her since she couldn't work if she wanted to be free to travel.

She wondered what Xander would be getting out of the deal, apart from the obvious use of her body. She didn't think he was the kind of man who normally paid for company. The way he made her feel as though she was the sexiest woman on the planet was a huge turn on, but she hardly knew him. Perhaps they could spend some time together getting to know each other before she committed to becoming his mistress. Everything was moving too fast and she needed more time to think. However, with funds running low and Nick about to be released, she was rapidly running out of time. Could she trust him? Would she be safe with him? The thoughts rushed around and around, crowding her brain, and when the car finally pulled to a stop she was no nearer to having made a decision.

Xander himself was there to open the car door, and she was delighted that he seemed to be as eager to see her, as she was to see him.

"Welcome to the Marquis, Chloe." He reached in to take her hand, drawing her out of the car and into his arms in one easy move.

He kissed her softly. His lips moved over hers slowly and gently as if she was precious. Enfolded in his arms, she felt safe and secure. No one would hurt her while she was with him. She realized with a start that she already trusted him to take care of her, and her body melted into his, as she surrendered to the security he promised.

Having kissed her thoroughly, he raised his head. His hand which had cupped her jaw as he kissed her, now brushed back a stray hair from her face.

"You look much better after your rest, sweetheart." He put his arm around her back and pulled her against his side, "Come, I will introduce you to my guests and then we can go into dinner."

"Where are we?" She tried looking around for clues, but apart from the large Gothic type building behind him, all she could see was countryside. The hotel, restaurant or whatever it was had no external signs; they could be at a private residence for all she knew.

He didn't stop as he strolled towards the entrance with her, "The Marquis. It's a country hotel and private club in Buckinghamshire. I'm a partner here," he told her, "and the clients we're having dinner with tonight are thinking of investing in the franchise; hence our reason for dining here and not in town."

"So, it's an important meeting?" she queried. Christ, she hoped she could cope! She hadn't imagined herself sitting in on a business dinner with potential investors. However, it would probably mean that he would behave himself and not make inappropriate suggestions during the meal if he had clients to impress. All she had to do was make polite small talk. Maybe she had been invited to keep the dinner from becoming too much of a business meeting.

"Nothing for you to worry your pretty little head about," he replied, bending low to whisper in her ear, his voice a throaty promise, "we'll have plenty of time for us after dinner."

Xander, however, was worried, even if he did not show it. He had not intended to bring her anywhere near the club just yet. Christ, he hadn't even discussed his lifestyle with her. He had wanted to introduce her to it slowly, behind closed doors. His playroom on the island would have been ideal. He had wanted her to get to know him better, to learn to trust him before he even mentioned anything like a scene.

Chloe had trust issues. Her history of abuse colored her judgment and made her wary. His stomach knotted as he remembered her reaction to his threatened spanking. He never wanted to see her that distraught again.

Having to entertain potential investors tonight was a real pain, but not something he had been able to get out of. Due to a family emergency Jake, his friend and one of his partners in the club chain, had been unable to meet the clients as arranged. Xander had been the only other partner, anywhere near the club, who could show the clients around. He would just have to make sure that he kept Chloe to the hotel side; he didn't want her running scared before he had a chance to talk to her about his lifestyle.

He introduced her to his guests, Kevan and Brad who were visiting from Australia. The business partners already ran a chain of successful up-market nightclubs and now wanted to branch out into the specialist BDSM scene. He noted the way Brad, the younger man, held her hand just a little longer than necessary. He would have to keep his eye on him tonight. He had a tendency to rush into things, to be a bit too rash, a fact he had noted earlier in the day during their discussions. It was the influence of Kevan, the elder of the two partners that kept Brad in line. Watching him as he lusted over Chloe, Xander felt irritated. Anger clawed at his throat and he battled with himself to remain silent. He struggled to relax his clenched fists as he fought back the intense resentment welling inside him. He needed to put a collar on her; brand her as his own. Having her here with no collar was asking for trouble, trouble he would have to head off.

He cursed himself for being selfish. He could have rearranged their dinner date for another night easily, but he had not wanted to wait another twenty-four hours to hold her again.

The night was still young and if he could wine, dine and shake off the clients quickly enough, he would have the rest of the evening to enjoy her. His body quickened at the thought and he looked forward to the night ahead. Being at the club had increased his appetite for her, and he could hardly wait until later when he would be able to remove her clothes at his leisure.

The dress he had sent her fit perfectly and highlighted her creamy complexion, the black lace a perfect foil for the blond hair that she had pinned up in an ornate twist with small tendrils of curls hanging loosely around her face. He was feeling very pleased with his decision to make her his mistress.

He noticed the looks his companions gave her, but to his delight, she paid them no heed, having eyes only for him. She had been polite to his guests, making nice with the social small talk, but had definitely kept her distance. He liked her reticence with the others and the fact that she did not flirt. When she joined in the conversation, her comments were intelligent and to the point though she rarely started a conversation herself.

He had concluded his business with his guests earlier in the day, so the talk around the dinner table had been convivial and more social than business. Brad, the younger of the two guests, had imbibed more freely of the drinks menu than the rest of them and was starting to get a little loud. A good reader of character, Xander studied him, aware that it was probably time to draw the dinner to a close before anything untoward came out.

"Well, gents, it's time we were off," Xander addressed the men at the table, as he reached out to draw Chloe to her feet.

"Not so early surely," Brad said, his voice slurred, "I still want to watch a few scenes before we call it a night!"

Xander held his breath and his grip on Chloe's hand tightened as he pulled her closer.

"Go, enjoy yourself." He gestured towards the other side of the room. "Chloe and I are going to call it a night. It's been a long day." He knew that Brad wouldn't get very far into the club; the security he employed was good and alcohol was frowned upon in the clubrooms. Drugs and alcohol did not mix in a BDSM club; safety was always paramount, only soft drinks were served within the club and anyone caught with drugs was banned for life. They operated a strict no tolerance policy.

Brad rose from his seat and lurched around the table towards them. He felt Chloe stiffen and draw closer to him, obviously feeling threatened.

For that alone he wanted to throttle the bastard, and when he reached out to grab her arm trying to pull her away from him, Xander felt violent.

"Come on babe," Brad tugged at her arm, "you and I can go and enjoy a scene or two."

Chloe looked between the two of them, unsure of what was going on. She didn't know what a 'scene' was, but thought it was probably Australian slang for dancing; she assumed the club was a nightclub. Embarrassed to be caught in the middle of an unseemly struggle, which brought back memories of her last meeting with Nick, she tried to diffuse the situation.

"Well, maybe we could go just for half an hour." She looked at Xander for confirmation that her acceptance was okay.

Shit. Now what was he going to do? "I don't think so Chloe," he replied, "we've got a long drive back to town." He'd not intended to go back to town tonight, but now he just wanted to get her out of here before everything blew up in his face. Moreover, if Brad, the asshole, didn't let go of her arm very soon, he was going to deck the bastard!

"Oh come on man, lighten up," Brad cut in.

At her side Xander tensed and she noticed his eyes narrow as he looked first at Brad and then at his hold on her arm. Her stomach churned and she held her breath. Memories of the jealous rages Nick had flown into if anyone so much as looked at her swept through her and she felt sick. Nick had always blamed her as if it was her fault, as if she had encouraged others to flirt with her. She wondered how Xander was going to react.

She took a deep breath and tried to control her trembling. She was surprised when Brad suddenly released his hold on her. He did not give up altogether though. "I'm sure Chloe would love to watch a scene or two." He winked at Xander. "Warm her up, if you get my drift."

Xander stayed perfectly still. She wondered if this was the calm before the storm. Would he lash out at Brad? Or her?

She could feel the undercurrent of simmering tension in the arm that Xander had around her waist. He had been obviously annoyed at the way Brad had grabbed her, but Brad had released her, so what was the problem? She didn't understand their conversation. She felt like there was something else going on, something she had missed.

"Fine," he snapped at Brad, "you and Kevan go ahead. Watch but no playing, you both know the alcohol rules." His tone brooked no argument.

"I need ten minutes with Chloe alone; I've not seen her all day. We'll catch up with you soon."

Xander had to get her away from them before one or the other said something untoward and she figured out exactly what kind of club they were visiting. Her brow was furrowed and she looked confused, but he was pleased to see that her color had improved. When Brad had first grabbed her arm the color had drained from her face leaving her pale. Did she not realize that he wouldn't let anyone hurt her?

"Come on, sweetheart," he spoke softly to her, "I need to pop up to the office for a few minutes."

He cuddled her close against his side as he steered her through the restaurant towards the back of the hotel where his office was located, not that he was there often enough to need a permanent office, but at times it proved useful.

"Xander, is everything alright?" Her voice was low and shaky, almost as if she feared his response. He felt like a bastard. He'd promised to protect her and yet here she was trembling because someone he had introduced her to had made a grab at her. At that moment, he could have cheerfully knocked Brad on his ass. He should have decked the swine.

"It will be," he returned cryptically, "if we ever get some time alone." His tone was brisk, but he cuddled her close, in an effort to reassure her.

He just needed more time with her, alone. He needed time to develop the intimacy and trust between them. Although he felt he knew her and he prided himself that he was very good at reading women, she didn't know him at all. There was no way she was ready for an introduction into the BDSM lifestyle. He was going to have to dissuade her from going any further into the club. After her reaction to the threat of a spanking, she was likely to run for the hills and refuse to have anything more to do with him. He should send her back to the hotel while he finished off business with Kevan and Brad.

He cursed silently under his breath. They had barely been together 48 hours and, now because of that asshole, he was going to have to explain a lot more to her than he had planned to at this stage. The last thing he wanted to do was frighten her. His lifestyle was supposed to be based on trust between partners, and he was feeling guilty that he hadn't been upfront with her so far. It was time to put his cards on the table; he only hoped she was strong and open minded enough to listen to what he had to say.

Chapter Six

Closing the door to the office behind them, he pinned her to the back of the door with her arms stretched above her head, as he lowered his body against hers.

"First things first, darling," he said as he lowered his head, "I just need a little taste before I go out of my mind."

He loved the way she responded to him, the way her body sagged as it melted into his, the little moans at the back of her throat as he kissed her. The way she tried to arch her body closer to him as his kiss deepened and he thrust his tongue deep, mimicking what he would like to be doing with his body. Panting heavily, he stepped back from her; he couldn't allow himself anymore, if he continued kissing her responsive lips he was going to end up taking things a hell of a lot further than he intended at the moment.

He needed to talk to her, prepare her for the club and give her an out if she didn't want to go and watch the scenes. He hoped she wouldn't opt out; he wanted to see her response to all the stimuli she would be presented with if she decided to accompany him. Her reactions to the various scenes would give him a far better understanding of her sexual nature than she would reveal otherwise.

Xander was sure that, to date, she had lived a completely vanilla sex life. She had seemed surprised at his taking control in bed, shocked when he had fingered her asshole and her reaction to the threat of spanking had spoken volumes. She had obviously never considered spanking as a form of erotic foreplay. But, her reaction to him and the very light control he had taken in bed, led him to believe that she might be open to giving up a bit more control. He wondered how much control he could persuade her to give up. His pulse raced at the thought of her total submission.

"Come and sit down a minute," he clasped her hand as he led her toward the chairs in front of his desk, "we need to have a chat before we join the others."

"Do you not want to join the others?" Her tone was reticent.

"Not tonight, particularly," he mused, "but they are clients and I'm supposed to be entertaining them for the evening. I suppose I will have to show my face. You, on the other hand, are not obliged to accompany me to into the club."

"Don't you want me to go with you?" She queried tremulously. She sounded hurt and unsure of herself and he cursed himself for bringing her here, for causing her to doubt him. It was the last thing he needed right now when he was still attempting to establish trust between them. He needed to reassure her, convince her that he still wanted her.

"I would like nothing more than to take you next door." Good God wasn't that the truth! "However, I think we need to discuss a few things first," he continued, "such as, whether or not you have decided to take up my offer."

"You mean the offer to become your mistress?" She blushed as she queried him.

"I wasn't aware I had made any other." He leaned back in the chair, attempting to relax, as he awaited her answer.

"I'm not sure, Xander," she whispered quietly. "Can't I have more time to think about it?"

He bit back a curse, surprised at her answer. "Impossible!" He was impatient, what the hell was there for her to think about? Any other woman would have jumped at the chance to be his mistress. He'd been sure she was going to accept his proposal, but it looked like a little persuasion was going to be needed. He needed to go and check up on Kevan and Brad, as he didn't want to leave them alone for too long. Nevertheless, it was important that he brought her around to his way of thinking. He would just have to spend a bit more time putting her fears to rest. He found himself wondering why women couldn't be more logical.

"Impossible? Why?"

"What don't you understand? It was a straightforward offer Chloe; you agree to become my mistress and I agree to become your protector, financially, emotionally and physically," his tone was clipped.

"Xander, please…" she pleaded with him, "it's not that I'm ungrateful, I just don't understand what you gain. I can see the benefits to myself, but what do you get out of the arrangement?"

"Me?" He winked, displaying more confidence than he felt. "I get you. I get every inch of your delectable body in my bed, as and when I want, however I want, whenever I want."

Her pupils flared, betraying her arousal at his words but then she turned away from him. She didn't look at him as she spent what felt like an eternity playing with the ends of her hair, twirling the strands around and around her fingers. He held his breath as he wondered if she was going to accept his proposal.

Lifting her head suddenly, she looked him straight in the face, blushing lightly as she asked, "And that's enough for you? That's all you want?"

He leaned forward in his seat and kissed her lightly, his fingers traveling back through the locks of her hair as he urged her closer. He whispered in her ear. "Access to your body and a signed confidentiality agreement will make me a very happy man, darling."

"What--" she pulled abruptly away to stare at him bewildered, "what the hell do you need a confidentiality agreement for?"

"A man in my position needs to be careful," he studied her closely. "I don't want a repeat of the last fiasco."

"What fiasco?"

Had she not been listening to him earlier in the day when he had explained about Marie? He stood up abruptly and walked around to sit at the other side of his desk. Facing her across the expanse of wood, not being able to touch her and reassure her was hell, but he had to make her realize how important this was to him.

Forearms resting on the leather blotter, he leaned towards her, keeping eye contact. He needed to assess her reactions as he spoke.

"As you don't appear to remember our earlier discussion I am going to give you a brief run down."

He held up his hand to silence her as she went to voice her objection, "No, listen to me. You need to hear this and this time, pay attention." His tone was serious as he continued, "My last relationship ended badly, my ex-girlfriend sold her story to the rag papers and celebrity gossip magazines; a real 'kiss and tell' exposé revealing our private life. I do not want, nor will I ever allow, that to happen again."

Her eyes widened as he reiterated his reason for wanting a confidentiality agreement between them.

"You think I would do that to you?" Her tone raised in shock. She was obviously annoyed and maybe a little offended.

He was surprised to realize that her offense didn't bother him. In fact, he felt quite smug that he had judged her morals correctly. Time would tell if his judgment was on the mark.

"I don't know, Chloe," Xander replied slowly, "That's why I insist on the agreement. I would like to think that I am a better judge of character now, but I don't know you very well yet, just as you don't know me."

"But, you still want to have an affair with me? Make me your mistress?"

"I very much want to have an affair with you," he stated unequivocally, "I relish the thought of us having more time together, of getting to know you better. But, I need the reassurance that there will not be a repeat of what happened before; I like to keep my private life just that, private!"

"In that case," she queried hesitantly, "do you not think it would be better if I just worked for you, for a while, just until we get to know each other better?"

Shit! No way. He wouldn't be able to touch her.

"No, I bloody well don't!" He replied through gritted teeth. "I'm not leaving myself open to a sexual harassment charge from an employee. You are either my mistress or nothing; so what is it to be?"

He knew he was pushing her, but hell, time was short and he had to return home. There was no way he was going to leave her behind with Nick about to be released. If she went with him, he would know she was safe. He didn't like backing her into a corner, but he knew full well that her options were limited.

They were good together. The chemistry between them was explosive and needed further exploration. He would have to stand his ground; it wouldn't work if she were an employee.

He walked around to the front of his desk, leaning back against it when he stopped directly in front of her chair, thinking maybe she'd respond to a bit of gentle persuasion. He reached out to take her hands to pull her out of the chair and up against him, letting her feel how much he wanted her. He cuddled her close, one hand cupping her bottom as the other caressed her nape.

"Look, Chloe, the agreement is no big deal for someone in my position. It just means that if and when we go our separate ways, when our affair has played itself out, you can't go selling your story. You will be well compensated for your agreement."

"You think I want your money?" She snapped, definitely offended now.

"No, I don't think you are after my money, but, I am after your body. I want the right to make you scream, to show you pleasure you haven't yet imagined, to make you mine." He knew he was being unfair, appealing to the sexual chemistry between them, but he didn't feel the least bit guilty. "I don't want to have to worry about you going to the papers with it afterward, what's so wrong with that?"

He knew he was getting through to her, as she relaxed and molded her body against him, obviously aroused.

"Well, when you put it that way," she lifted her head and gave him a wicked grin, "maybe I am being a little silly. After all, I know I won't go to the papers with a story. You've got to learn to trust me."

He released a breath he hadn't realized he had been holding. Yes! She was going to sign, he could feel it.

He felt like a bastard when he saw her dismay as he glanced at his watch. He really didn't want to leave his guests too long on their own. God knew what they would get up to.

He dipped his head and kissed her hard, just to let her know who was in charge in their relationship, and was instantly rewarded by a small moan. He turned swiftly, so that their positions were reversed and she had his desk at her rear, he lifted her to sit on the desk all the while not breaking their kiss. He stepped between her open legs, then, eased her back on the desk beneath him. Holding her arms at the wrists, he spread them wide as he surveyed her from top to bottom. Removing his hands he said, "Don't move, keep your arms where they are," as he held her in position with his stare, "I just want to look at you for a moment." He wanted to do a lot more than look, but first he had to get the agreement signed and then he had to go into the club.

Frustration gnawed at his gut. He had been semi-erect ever since she'd stepped out of the car wearing the short black dress. He'd spent half the evening fantasizing about getting her out of it. She was laid across his desk, his for the taking, and he had to walk away and leave her alone. He silently cursed his friend Jake and hoped he appreciated the sacrifice he had made for the sake of their business.

"You are absolutely gorgeous," he told her, "and I am so looking forward to taking you home with me. I can hardly wait to watch you come apart, to hear you scream when you cum, baby girl."

He laughed with delight as he saw the blush suffuse her body. It amazed him that after everything they had already done together that she could still be shy with him.

"Much as I would love to take you hard, here and now," he was being wicked and he knew it, but couldn't resist when he saw how her pupils had flared in arousal, "I have to go and find Kevan and Brad and make sure they're not up to any mischief. We will have to wait until later, sweetheart."

He leaned over to kiss her gently, once again grasping her hands, only this time he pulled her up into a sitting position. He pulled the contract he had already had his lawyers draw up from his jacket pocket and presented it to her with a pen.

"The contract?" She queried, nibbling her lip. "You already had it drawn up?"

"I like to be prepared. Sit here, take your time to read it and if you're happy with it, sign it." He lifted her off the desk and placed her back in the chair she had recently vacated. "I'm going to nip into the Club and make sure the boys are alright, I'll be back shortly so don't go anywhere. If there's anything in that," he nodded to the contract in her hand, "that you don't understand or any questions you have, we can discuss it when I get back." He walked out, leaving her in his office to peruse the document, confident that she would stay there until he got back.

Chloe couldn't believe she had given in to his demands so easily. He only had to touch her and she went up in flames, and common sense went out of the window.

What had happened to all her great ideals? What had happened to the serious talk she was going to have with him, to persuading him that it would be better if she took the job instead of becoming his mistress? Xander had happened, she just couldn't resist his rugged charm or deny herself access to his body. Still, now that she had agreed to accompany him as his mistress she had better take a look at this contract he had drawn up.

She went around the desk to sit in his high back leather chair. She could imagine him there, overseeing staff with masterly control. He was definitely a man who would take his responsibilities seriously and who wouldn't suffer fools. The office was like the man himself, the furniture large, strong and very masculine. The furniture dominated the room, just like the man dominated her.

Slowly she opened the contract, pressing it flat against the desk as she bent to read the fine print. He had to be joking. He couldn't seriously expect her to agree to all these conditions. Amazement coursed through her as she re-read it, trying to assimilate everything it contained. God only knows what the poor stenographer who had typed it had thought. Was nothing private?

Every aspect of the life he envisioned living with her had been mapped out and accounted for. He had outlined where they would live, how often they would travel and the way he expected her to comport herself. The document contained a list of his requirements with regard to their day-to-day lives. He expected her to exercise, to sleep at regular times, to dress in the clothes he provided. It also contained a confidentiality clause and outlined whom she was allowed to discuss their agreement with. She could talk to a physician, appointed by Xander and her own lawyer. She was not permitted to reveal details of their arrangement to anyone else. She was expressly forbidden to talk to any media outlet about their relationship.

The contents of the document took her by surprise. She had been expecting a standard employment type contract that laid out terms and conditions. She had not been expecting a contract that went into so much detail and very personal detail at that. She had read with disbelief that he would provide her with a new wardrobe. When she came across the part where he laid down the rules for eating and sleeping times, she felt angry. Upon reaching his conditions, re disclosure of their relationship, she had had enough and discarded the contract to one side. It was obviously a lot more than a standard employment contract. If she agreed to the terms it contained, it would be like signing her life away. She wondered if all wealthy people entered into relationships in this manner. It certainly wasn't the norm in her own circle; neither was asking someone to become your mistress and insisting on a contract to that effect. Did he not trust anyone? Surely, there had to be more than an ex-girlfriend selling her story to the papers to make him so untrusting, so controlling.

She needed a better explanation as to why he needed to control every aspect of their lives. She needed to know how he would react when things didn't go according to his plans. Was he likely to get angry as Nick had, or go with the flow? Would his need for control allow him to be spontaneous?

She thought back to how they had met, and how he had solicited her as his mistress. There was no way he could have planned for their meeting; it had been purely chance that he had met her at the hotel. Moreover, she gave a little giggle amused at the thought; there is no way he could have planned for having her as his mistress. It pleased her that she had gotten under his skin and forced him to deviate from his plan. After all, he had her acting completely out of character.

Reading the contract, however, what did shine through was his complete lack of trust, it was written between the lines in the passages that outlined the confidentiality he expected. Did he really think she was capable of going to the press with a story about their bedroom antics? She wouldn't cause herself the embarrassment.

Unable to settle she wandered around his office, gliding her hands across the highly polished and beautifully crafted wooden furniture; it was very tactile, warm and strong. Like Xander, she mused. It suited him far better than any modern chrome or plastic would have. Browsing his bookcase, she saw several books on cabinet making and various Do-It-Yourself books on the use of different woodworking tools. It was the first evidence she had seen that he took his work as a craftsman seriously. If she had not already known that he was a craftsman from the advert, she would never have guessed from the way he fit into the role of the wealthy executive. He was just too urban, too smooth, and altogether too sharp to fit her image of a woodworker. She had expected someone a little bohemian, quite a bit older, who wore casual clothes, worn blue jeans and faded flannel shirts. She had not been prepared at all for Xander, suave, good looking, wearing designer garb, full of charm and wealthy beyond her imagining.

Glancing at her watch, she realized that he had been gone for nearly half an hour. She was contemplating going in search of him, when he returned. Closing the door behind him, Xander leaned back against the wood, as he looked her over.

"Did you sign the agreement?" He was watching her warily.

"No."

He raised his eyebrow in query. "What was in it that you didn't like?"

"Well, let's see…," she started, "for one, there's the matter of you supplying my clothes." She held up the finger on one hand, "Two…" she paused to hold up another finger, "there is the point where you dictate my eating, sleeping and exercise routine." Now that had really annoyed her. Just who the hell did he think he was? Those rules had made him sound more like her father than her prospective lover.

"Most women would love to have a new designer wardrobe supplied for them." Leaning back against the door with his arms crossed nonchalantly, he had the nerve to wink at her, "No expense spared."

It wasn't the expense she was thinking about, more the fact that he was dictating what she would wear. Nick, her ex, had become more and more obsessed with what she wore. She hadn't been able to wear anything he deemed too short, too tight, too low cut or figure hugging. She had caved into his demands in an effort to keep the peace and, ultimately, out of fear of his reaction as his jealousy and possessiveness escalated. For many months prior to their break-up, she had dressed in clothes picked out by him. The outfits he had chosen, had been designed for older women, and she'd felt dowdy. Well, she had been down that road before, and she wasn't treading that path again, not for Xander, not for anybody.

"I'm not most women!" she snapped, "I don't want you dictating what I wear. I'm pretty grown up, Xander, a big girl," she emphasized, "perfectly capable of dressing myself."

"Oh, you're all grown up alright, darling," he drawled, "I can testify to that!" He had the nerve to stand there with a wicked grin across his face, as he surveyed her slowly from head to toe, not in the least taking her concerns seriously.

"Xander, be serious." How the hell was she going to get through to him? "Didn't what I told you about Nick register at all?" She queried.

"I'm nothing like that asshole!" Came his quick response, but he was serious all of a sudden. Straightening away from the door, he walked slowly toward her, his eyes intent on her face. He came to a halt a couple of feet in front of her.

"I will never tell you what you can or cannot wear. I am providing a new wardrobe because I do a lot of entertaining and I want you to feel comfortable." He went on, "The people I mix with are wealthy; all their wives and girlfriends will be wearing designer clothes. My aim was to help you fit in without having to go to the expense on your own."

Put like that, she felt churlish refusing his offer. "Oh, I see…" she didn't know what else to say.

"So, now you understand, you will accept my offer?"

"Not so fast, Xander," she replied. "What about the other points I raised?"

"Other points?"

"Yes. The eating, sleeping and exercise routines your damn contract maps out."

"Well, they are for your own good." His voice was solemn. "I promised to look after you emotionally, physically and financially. It is up to me to see that you have enough rest, eat properly and keep yourself fit and healthy." He was looking at her slightly puzzled as if she should already understand this. "Would I not be neglecting you if I didn't ensure your welfare?"

"Do I look like a two-year-old?" She couldn't keep the anger out of her voice.

He appeared startled. "Of course you don't look like at two-year-old and I'm not looking for a Daddy type relationship!"

"Then stop treating me like a child. I'm perfectly capable of deciding when I want food. I'm perfectly capable of making myself a meal. I'm also," she continued, her voice rising as she strove to get her point across, "fully able to decide my own bedtimes."

"I apologize." His voice was low but rang with sincerity. "It wasn't my intention to make you feel belittled. The terms outlined in detail were meant to assure you of my intention to look after you, to give you confidence in my ability to take care of you." He looked confused as if he couldn't understand her objections.

Damn the man, he made it all sound so reasonable as if it was perfectly normal to draw up a contract at the start of a relationship. Then again, with his trust issues, maybe it was. Chloe started to feel sorry for him. It must be hard not to be able to trust those with whom you had even the closest of relationships.

"Do you trust me to take care of you, Chloe?"

Did she trust him? She thought about it for a moment as he stood patiently awaiting her answer. Did she have a choice? She still needed to leave London before Nick's release and Xander was offering her the only way out. Did it really matter that it was only on his terms, she pondered, if he was offering her the escape she needed? The contract had come as a surprise. However, as she had never been an official mistress before, was it really so out of the ordinary? She wasn't signing her life away by agreeing to be his mistress for twelve months. This was the minimum period, stipulated within the contract, at the end of which she could walk away with a healthy bank balance, and no recriminations.

If she wasn't happy with their life, she could call it quits anytime she wanted though under those circumstances there would be no payoff.

"I suppose so, but--"

"No 'buts' Chloe. I would be negligent in my duty to care for you if I didn't ensure your total well-being. All I want to do is look after you."

"Maybe so, however, did you also have to put in a clause about our love life?" When she had read his clause regarding their sex life she had been more than annoyed. He wanted to guard his privacy but what about her own. There was no clause stating that he could not discuss their private life when the relationship ended. She had also suffered media scrutiny in the past and was not prepared to undergo such speculation again.

The clause with regard to their private lives had thrown her. His demand for sexual control was vague and unsettling. The contract gave no details and she nibbled on her lower lip as she wondered exactly what kind of control he wanted.

The sexual clauses that had been included were quite specific. By signing the contract, she would be agreeing to give him total control in the bedroom and in all sexual situations. She was not allowed to discuss their sex life with anyone other than a doctor, if necessary, and even then only with a doctor appointed by Xander. Again, it expressly forbade talking to any media outlet, publisher, ghost author, or writing her own memoirs that included private details of their sexual encounters.

"I explained my reasons for that clause earlier." His tone suggested that there was no way he would remove it. "I will not go through a fiasco like the last time again."

"What exactly do you mean by 'control in the bedroom and in all sexual situations' Xander?" Chloe was wary.

"I mean," he stepped forward to wrap his arms around her, as he bent his head to whisper in her ear, "that I will wear the pants in this relationship. That I will decide when and where I take you to bed, I will decide when you will gain your release and that all the pleasure that you feel will belong to me."

Oh God, she was going to dissolve in a puddle of need. Listening to him whisper in her ear, the pleasure that he promised was enough to have her insides trembling, and already she could feel moisture pooling between her thighs. Wrapped in his arms, surrounded by the feel of his muscular body and with his scent pervading her every pore, she was powerless to resist him.

He didn't play fair and she was helpless and unable to resist any longer. She snuggled closer, burrowing her face into his jacket. "Okay, you win."

"Look at me, Chloe." He grasped her jaw gently as he raised her head to place a light kiss in the middle of her forehead, "Good girl, I promise you will not regret your decision. I will take very good care of you."

He led her back to the desk where the contract lay opened and unsigned, without another word he picked up and handed her his pen. Quickly, before she changed her mind yet again, Chloe signed the contract and then watched as Xander calmly took it from her hands and walked across the room to lock it in his wall safe. Once the safe was locked, he turned to her all smiles, the tension seemed to have eased completely from his body.

"Well then darling, now that the business side of things is out of the way," he approached her with a swagger and a wide smile on his face, "I think it's time we had some fun."

"Are we going to the club?"

Suddenly he didn't look so comfortable and his approach toward her slowed.

"We could," he said slowly, as he watched her warily, "but it depends on you." He reached out to grasp her hands and pull her toward him.

"Why?" She was puzzled as to why he was making such an issue out of going dancing,

"Don't you want to go dancing?"

"It's not a nightclub, Chloe."

"Oh." She was momentarily at a loss, "What kind of club is it then?"

She watched as he took a deep breath, for once he didn't look as sure of himself as usual. If she didn't know better she would think he was worried about her possible response.

"It's a fetish club." He said quickly.

Oh shit, she hadn't seen that one coming. His face gave nothing away as he watched her reaction closely.

"You mean a sex club? A place they run orgies, do wife swaps and stuff like that?" Aghast, she tried to pull her hands free as she backed away from him, what kind of mess had she gotten herself into now? She looked toward the locked safe. Was it too late to retrieve and cancel the contract?

He held her hands tight, resisting her efforts to pull away from him.

"Shit, no," he replied. "It's nothing like that! Well, maybe it is, sometimes; but only if people want to." His explanation left a lot to be desired and the muscles in her stomach knotted in protest. Something wasn't right. She could feel it. Senses on alert, she struggled to control the trembling of her body. She had to have a better explanation.

"What do you mean maybe it is? It either is or it isn't, Xander." The butterflies in her stomach took flight and she heard her own voice tremble as she asked the question.

"Come and sit down and we'll talk about it. I'll explain if you give me a chance."

Relieved to be given a chance to sit down, she nodded in agreement. He didn't release her hands; instead, he led her to a small two-seat couch sat at a right angle to his desk. Still holding onto one hand, as though he didn't want to let her go, or didn't trust her not to run, he pulled up an office chair so that he was sitting knee to knee facing her.

"Eyes on me, sweetheart." Once again, he was back in command. He appeared so calm as if the bombshell he had thrown her way was of no consequence. Oddly, however, instead of feeling annoyed, she was reassured by his confident tone. She wondered at his ability to put her at ease. "I'm going to explain the club scene and how it works here. Just listen and if you have any questions, you can ask when I have finished. Okay?"

She cast her eyes over him. He no longer looked uncomfortable. He looked sure of himself, and a whole lot more confident than she felt. Discovering they were in a fetish club had astounded her. Now that she'd had a few moments to absorb the idea, her interest was piqued. She wanted to know what went on behind the closed doors. She would never admit it to him, but she was a little excited. Moreover, she reminded herself, she had already signed his contract.

Unable to trust her voice, she nodded in agreement.

She listened, mesmerized by his voice, as he explained the BDSM lifestyle in quite a detailed way; the different fetishes, the roles of Dominant and submissive, voyeurism, exhibitionism, sadists, and masochists. He went on to detail the facilities at the club, the safety measures put into place to ensure that the BDSM rules of Safe, Sane, and Consensual sex were always upheld. He explained the public and private rooms, the rooms for display and putting on scenes, the rules safeguarding members' privacy. He also explained that most relationships within the scene were monogamous and between committed couples.

All the time he was talking to her, he caressed her inner wrists with the pads of his fingers. He watched her closely and she felt as if her reactions were being carefully assessed.

"Any questions?"

Christ, she had hundreds, she just didn't know where to start, what to ask first. Maybe if they went next door she could get the answers for herself. Was she brave enough to take that step?

"If…. If we go into the club," she stammered, "Will I have to do anything?"

"Not tonight. Not ever, if you don't want to," he assured her gently. "We could just have a quiet look around, maybe watch a couple of displays and let you get a feel for the place."

"That's all, just look around?" She double-checked wanting to make sure she wasn't committing herself to anything else by agreeing to enter the club. The idea of viewing a live scene, without being obliged to participate, was kind of exciting and scary all at the same time.

"That's all," he promised as his hands came up to cup her face. "I'll be with you all the time, Chloe. Nobody but me will ever touch you."

"You're sure?" Little tremors of apprehension were coursing through her, but somehow she knew she would be safe with him.

"I promise Chloe. There's nothing to be afraid of. If you don't enjoy it just tell me and we will leave whenever you are ready." He sounded calm and very sincere as if she had no reason to worry.

"Okay."

"Okay? " He tilted his head to one side, a slight quizzical expression on his face and he continued to watch her. "Does that mean you want to visit the club now? You know it doesn't have to be this evening, we can always come back another time."

"No!" Her response was swift. "We're here now, so if I'm going to visit I would rather just go." In truth, she wasn't sure that if she didn't go now, she would ever have the courage to come back again.

"Fine," he nodded his head in agreement, "but be prepared. Tonight is 'leather and lace' night so most of the subs are wearing very little. I don't want you taken by surprise."

He stood, pulling her to her feet as he rose. "Come on baby girl, time to start your education." He grinned broadly. "The Marquis club awaits your pleasure."

Chapter Seven

Xander could hardly wait to see her reaction to the club and its patrons. He quickly ushered her past security. Normally all entrants had to be signed 'in and out' by the security staff, who at the same time would check them for alcohol and drugs, neither of which was permitted on the premises.

As Xander was part owner, he did not have to go through this ritual and therefore neither did his companion.

"Evening, Master X," the head of security greeted him as he nodded toward the public room entrance. "It's fairly quiet in there; most are up on the viewing floor tonight watching scenes and a demonstration that is going on."

Chloe looked at him in surprise, and as they moved away from the security personnel she whispered, "He called you Master X, what's that all about?"

He cast a sideways glance, noting her faintly shocked expression. "Chloe, were you not listening when I explained about Dominant/submissive roles?"

"Yes, I was," she reassured him, "only you didn't mention anything about being a Dom. I would have remembered that!"

He closed his eyes and took a deep breath. Maybe he had not explained things clearly enough. He was exasperated with himself, but the foyer of the club where he could be overhead by his staff, was hardly the place to go into another detailed discussion. He kept his voice low in the hope that only she could hear him. "And you're trying to tell me it never crossed your mind, even knowing that I like to be in control?"

"Well, hmm...," she was looking at him wide eyed, "well that's different; it doesn't make you one of them!" She sounded shocked. Her eyes had grown wide and she deliberately kept her distance from him as if she was no longer sure she could trust him.

He stopped to look at her, turning her toward him in order to read her expression. She was looking at him with a mixture of fear and excitement, almost as if she hoped he wasn't involved in the lifestyle but maybe, secretly, she was wishing that he was. He couldn't decide which emotion was winning; she nibbled her bottom lip nervously as she returned his stare.

"One of them?" He questioned quietly, a little disappointed at her response, "We're not lepers, Chloe."

She backed away from him, freeing her hand from his hold as she ran the palms of her hands down her sides, straightening her dress, as if she was suddenly conscious of how short it was.

"Maybe not lepers, but it's definitely not normal," she continued, a fearful look on her face. "Its not normal to want to hurt someone else, to want to inflict pain."

"Who said anything about pain?" Not giving her a chance to reply, he queried, "Do you know that there are different types of pain? Do you know that some pain can be very erotic?"

She looked at him skeptically. "You'll be telling me pigs can fly next!"

"Look," he reasoned with her, "I'm not going to force you to accompany me, the choice is yours." He reached toward her, inviting her to take his hand. "If you do decide to come in with me, you must keep your opinions to yourself. We have a very select clientele here, who come because they enjoy having somewhere to play without censure or ridicule. They don't come here to be criticized, especially," he emphasized, "by someone who doesn't know what she's talking about!"

"Well--" Her voice bristled with indignation and she made no effort to take his outstretched hand.

"That's non-negotiable, Chloe," he told her firmly, "if you have questions you can ask me later. When we are alone."

He wanted to laugh at the look on her face. She was all wounded pride and indecision, as she twisted the strands of her hair around her fingertips. She would never make a poker player; her face gave away her every thought. He stood, waiting patiently, making no move to influence her decision. She had to learn that the choice was always hers and that he would abide by her decision. Her internal struggle was clear. He could almost hear the cogs ticking. On the one hand, he could tell she was outraged to find herself in such a place. At the same time, her eyes were glowing with excitement. He could tell she was tempted by the forbidden pleasures she perceived were behind the doorway.

He knew when she'd reached her decision. She stood up straighter and looked him straight in the eye as she nodded her head. "Okay." She grasped his hand tightly. "Let's go. Nothing ventured, nothing gained."

"Brave girl," he murmured, as he leaned down and kissed her softly. "Remember, we're only here to be social. We'll mingle for half an hour, take in a scene or two, there's nothing for you to worry about."

He led her through the double doors into the public area. Scanning the area he spotted a booth on the opposite wall that was unoccupied, and he headed across the room to claim it. He would get her settled where she could look around discreetly. It would let her get a feel for the place.

She held onto his hand tightly, as if afraid to let go of him. Reaching the booth, he ushered her into it before sliding in to sit beside her.

"You can open your eyes now," he teased. He couldn't keep the humor from his voice. He would bet his last dollar that she had kept her eyes glued to the floor as they had crossed the room.

Her head snapped up and she eyed him warily, "I have not got my eyes shut!" Nevertheless, she looked nowhere other than directly at him, as she nibbled on her bottom lip.

"Not now, maybe," he teased, leaning in quickly to nip her bottom lip gently, "but I still reckon you took nothing in when we crossed the room."

She swiped the tip of her tongue across her now swollen lip, "Well, it's fairly dark in here, so that's not surprising."

"Well now you can just sit back, relax and have a look around. Let your eyes adjust while I go to the bar and get us a drink."

"I thought there was a no alcohol rule?"

"There is an alcohol limit rule, two and no more if you're taking part in a scene." He added wickedly, "But, as you won't indulge me I…"

"No way!" She sat up straighter as she glowered at him.

He loved it when she got feisty. He would love it even more if she could be persuaded to turn that passion in another direction altogether.

"Well then, I'll go and get the drinks. You stay there. Be good until I get back."

Huh, good until he got back. What the hell did he think she was going to get up to? Chloe sat back, trying to relax, as she watched Xander cross the room to the bar. Occasionally he stopped to chat to others, men that he obviously knew if the grins and handshakes were any indication. He stood out like a beacon in the room, and not just, because he appeared to be the only one dressed in a suit. People seemed to gravitate towards him and his progress to the bar was slow.

There sure were some good-looking men around, most of which were wearing leather pants. Tight leather pants that left very little to the imagination. A few also sported leather waistcoats, over their bare chests. No more than a couple wore shirts with their pants. All exuded an air of confidence that was apparent in the way they held themselves. The air was full of so much testosterone she could almost taste it. Shit, she had never seen so many alpha males together in her life!

Losing sight of Xander in the crowd, she turned her attention to the dance floor were several couples were gyrating to the music. Tina Turners' 'Private Dancer' was belting out of the sound system. She was shocked at how scantily clad some of the girls were. They wore no more than lace underwear or very diaphanous baby doll dresses with nothing more than a thong underneath. She remembered Xander telling her that tonight was 'leather and lace' night at the club. Christ, did the girls have no shame! Most nights, she wore more to go to bed.

One couple in particular caught her attention and she watched, mesmerized by their blatant display. The girl wore a white, sheer and very short negligee with a minute thong. Her long dark hair hung down her back in a braid. She undulated up against her partner, turning her back on him, and bending forward as she pushed her bottom against his crotch suggestively. Catching her braid, which he wrapped around his hand, her partner pulled her up against him. Chloe caught her breath at the blatantly sexual power play, unable to tear her gaze away she wondered what would come next.

She watched in fascination as the Dom pulled his partner, from the dance floor to an adjacent seating area by her braid. As he sat down, he ordered her to her knees between his outstretched legs before unbuttoning his leather pants, letting his erect penis bob out. "Suck me." Chloe lip-read his instructions across the room. No! Surely, she wouldn't.

Unable to tear her gaze away, she watched in horrified fascination. The girl bent forward to place her lips around his erection. As the girl's head bobbed up and down the length of him, Chloe watched him fight to control his release. Surely, they could not get away with putting on such a display. She scanned the room quickly, looking for security personnel. Was nobody going to do anything? Christ, anywhere else they would be charged with public indecency.

Turning back to look at the couple, she was just in time to see him withdraw from the sub's mouth before he spurted his cum across her now naked breasts. Her breath hitched in shock. As if he had heard her gasp, he looked directly at her and winked. She felt the blush suffuse her face and quickly looked away, only to come face to face with Xander who stood to the side of the booth watching her. It was plain from the grin on his face that he had witnessed her fascination. She felt like a voyeur caught in the act. The heat of her embarrassment coursed through her and she felt her face flush. Her face wasn't the only part of her body flushing, and she wriggled in her seat as she tried to soothe the ache between her legs. The blatant display had turned her on and she fought to hide her reaction. There was no way she wanted him to know that the scene had aroused her, she didn't want him getting ideas of his own. She was definitely, no exhibitionist.

He placed their drinks on the table before sliding into the booth, crowding her into the corner out of view.

"Enjoy that little show, kitten?" She was mortified that he had caught her enjoying the show, and she could not bring herself to meet his gaze.

"It was indecent." She took a sip of her wine, replacing the glass on the table before she continued, "He more or less dragged her off the dance floor and made her go down on him. Nobody even tried to stop him!"

"Why would they? He's her Dom. If he wants her on her knees, then on her knees she will go."

She couldn't understand it and replayed the scene in her head. She wondered why the girl would allow herself to be treated like that in public. It certainly wasn't for her. Nevertheless, she admitted to herself, she had found it very arousing to watch.

He placed his finger under her chin forcing her to look at him. "She had the choice, kitten. She can say no anytime she wants and he will respect her wishes."

"I bet!"

"That's the rule of the game, honey." He was being serious now. "The submissive has all the power. She only has to safe word and everything stops. Any Dom who doesn't obey that rule is being abusive and will be charged with assault. He would certainly never be allowed in here to play again."

Rules? The thought flashed through her mind. She looked at him astounded, hardly able to believe they actually had rules that covered the kind of scene she had just witnessed.

"You're trying to tell me she wanted to do that?" Her tone was scathing.

"Sure," he nodded over to where the couple were now cuddling, "does she look like she's upset about it?"

"Well, no..."

"Then, what's your problem?"

She felt confused. The other people in the club obviously had no problem with what had just occurred; in fact, most hadn't even given the other couple a second glance. It was all so different from what she was used to and from what she accepted as normal. Watching the scene had been a turn-on, but she had also felt like she was being naughty and intruding on what should have been a private moment. She wondered if Xander thought she was a prude.

"Oh, I don't know," she watched Xander closely as she replied, "it just seemed so blatant. Anywhere else they would have been charged with indecency."

"Maybe so, but that's why we have clubs like this and playrooms at home. No one should have to be ashamed of their sexuality." The muscle at the side of his jaw throbbed betraying his emotional response to her questions. "What's so wrong with the human form that people can't accept nakedness or want to keep lovemaking hidden?"

"But some things are private, Xander. Not meant for public consumption." Her stomach churned and her hands suddenly felt clammy as she recalled his earlier comment about sexual control. Surely, he didn't believe in performing in front of others.

"True, baby girl," he bit out, "but that doesn't stop some people trying to exploit others. The little display you just witnessed wasn't about exploitation. It was about a couple giving in to their need of each other."

"Well, they could have done that privately!"

"Why should they? To protect your sensibilities, when you mean nothing to them?" His tone was harsh with disapproval. "It's up to them how they conduct their sex life, and this club is here to allow them to express themselves however they want. We are not here to censor people."

"Well, I still don't agree with it."

"Maybe not," the look he gave her was appraising, "but I bet it turned you on just the same."

"How can you say that?" She snapped.

"Easily, kitten. You're all flushed, your eyes are dilated, your nipples are clearly budding," he put out his hand to cup a breast as his thumb brushed over her nipple, "and I have no doubt at all that your panties are wet."

She brushed his hand away, embarrassed that he could read her so well. Shit, could she hide nothing from him? It was true, watching the sub give her Dom pleasure had been a turn on. She didn't understand her feelings. How could something that struck her as abusive also strike her as very erotic? Aware that her confusion might show in her eyes, she turned away from him, determined to change to the subject.

"So, what other treats do you have in store for me tonight?"

"You mean," he asked, "that after all your indignation, you are willing to stay a bit longer? I thought you would want to leave."

"Mm.... No, I don't want to leave." She turned to look directly at him as she stated rebelliously, "I said I would look around with you and I will. I keep my word. So what's next?"

Xander was amused at her tone. She had surprised him and not many people were capable of that. Having voiced her indignation at the little sex scene she had witnessed, he had expected her to demand to be taken home. She had to be feeling a little off balance. Being completely new to the scene and only having experienced vanilla sex, he hadn't expected her to agree so readily to continue to explore the club.

"Well, if you're sure—"

"I've already said I am," she snapped, cutting him off. Her feisty attitude turned him on, and he looked forward to the day when he could get her to channel it in a more pleasurable direction. He could see that he was going to have his work cut out to train her and his pulse raced at the challenges ahead.

"Right then, there's a couple of demonstrations going on, on the upper level. Let's see what you make of them."

He held her hand firmly as he guided her through the crowded bar. Taking the stairs up from the main foyer, he led her to a private viewing room. He wasn't going to risk taking her to a public viewing, as he wasn't sure, how she would react to the demonstration about to commence. He also wanted no distractions to take his focus away from her. He needed to keep his mind focused on Chloe and her reactions, not worry about others around them.

"Here we are, Sweetheart." He opened a door off the main corridor and ushered her into a small room. Rather like a private box at the theatre, each side of the room was sealed off from the adjoining room, and the front overlooked a small stage. A stage which at this moment was currently set up to resemble a bedroom, complete with all the necessary furniture as well as a few pieces he felt sure that Chloe wouldn't recognize.

Closing the door behind them, Xander pulled her into his arms for a quick kiss, before releasing her and pointing to the seating. Unlike normal theatre seats, the booth contained a chaise longue and a couple of love seats. "Get yourself settled, the demo will start shortly."

"What kind of demo are we going to see?" she asked, the slight tremble in her voice betraying her nervousness.

"Be patient." He threw her a wink. "You'll soon find out."

He didn't want to tell her, just in case she walked out before the event even started. He was feeling apprehensive about her reaction after her outrage at the little kink she had witnessed on the dance floor. Christ that had been no more than vanilla sex in public. Nevertheless, he reminded himself, it had turned her on. Maybe there was hope for him yet. He'd not intended to bring her anywhere near the club at this stage in their relationship. However, fate, in the form of Brad and Kevan, had intervened. He wasn't about to let the opportunity slip by. He reasoned with himself that he had tried to talk her out of attending the club, he'd warned her what to expect, yet she had insisted on accompanying him. Perhaps, he thought, it would be better to let her see exactly what he enjoyed. He could hardly wait to see how she would react to something she might consider less normal.

"Comfy?" he asked, once she was seated. He noted with amusement that she had avoided the chaise and had instead opted for a love seat. *No chance of getting horizontal on that.*

"Yes, fine." She turned to look over the stage set, before turning back to ask, "How long before this demo starts?"

He glanced at his watch, as he took the adjoining seat. "Not long. It will probably be in the next five minutes or so." He had no sooner said the words, than the stage lights flickered on and off, announcing the arrival of the demonstrators on the stage.

Xander slipped his arm around Chloe's shoulder.

Chapter Eight

Chloe snuggled closer, enjoying the feel of being in his arms. Cocooned in their private little room, she struggled to contain the urge to do more than cuddle. It was less than twelve hours since he had last made love to her, but she wanted him again. She was fast becoming addicted to his brand of possession. His arm was strong and he held her firmly. She felt safer than she had in a long time.

The bravado she had put on when insisting she accompany him into the club had about deserted her now. Bloody hell! What had she gotten herself into this time? She couldn't believe she was about to watch a live sex demo. She had never done anything like this. Apprehension coursed through her body, and she made a conscious effort to relax her tense muscles. She didn't want to disappoint him. She was curious. Who wouldn't be? But with him right next to her she was also embarrassed. How the hell was she going to look him in the face when it was over?

"Ladies and gentlemen, Dominants and submissives, welcome." The man took center stage and addressed his audience. "Tonight we are going to give a small demo on bondage. It is important that you know what you are doing when you choose this kind of play, in order that you cause no lasting harm."

Chloe was surprised at the topic. She had been expecting something far more sexual, not some lesson in restraint techniques. Well, this shouldn't be too bad. She gave a small sigh of relief. She might feel indignation on behalf of the girl being restrained, but she was unlikely to be embarrassed.

"I am Master Damien," the man on stage announced himself, "and the subs helping out with tonight's demonstration are Kayla and Sabrina." Both the girls gave a small bow to the theater but said nothing.

"The first thing you must do before restraining your sub, is make sure that you have his or her agreement." Damien looked around the audience, his tone completely serious. "Failure to get consent will leave you open to a charge of abuse. For subs in the audience, make sure you trust your partner 100% before you give that consent because once you're tied up, there's not an awful lot you can do."

Chloe contemplated how she would feel if she were tied up and at Xander's mercy. Surprisingly, the idea set off a tremor of delicious tingles as she imagined him paying worship to her body. She was confused by her own reaction and twirled a strand of hair around and around her finger, as she tried to work out why the idea turned her on.

Xander grasped her hand, unwinding the strands of hair from between her fingers, before enveloping her much smaller hand within his own.

"Stop looking so worried, sweetheart," he whispered in her ear. "Keep your eyes on the stage. These demo's are not called lessons for nothing. Watch and learn."

It was almost as if he had read her thoughts.

Damien continued. "Ensure before you start playing with any form of restraint that you have agreed upon a safeword. If you are going to be using any form of gag, then make sure you have agreed on a safe signal. Take a tip from me, your partner needs to know that she can call a halt or get your attention in some other way when she wants. It is advisable to have some form of clear signal, for example, a bright colored golf ball which your sub can hold. If she drops the ball you will see it, you will hear it and if she throws it at you, you will definitely feel it." He laughed at his own little joke. "Now that we've established that basic rule, let's have a look at some of the more common forms of restraint."

He motioned Kayla to step forward in order that the audience had a good view. "Wrist and ankle cuffs are the most popular choices with many who choose this type of play." Kayla held up her arms and shook a leg, demonstrating the leather cuffs she already wore.

"If you look closely at Kayla's cuffs you will see that they are soft leather. You need to ensure they fit your partner snugly, but you should still be able to slip a finger in between the cuff and the sub's skin." Damien slipped a couple of fingers easily under the cuff on Kayla's wrist and ran them around under the leather binding. The cuffs appeared slack enough to be comfortable, but not so loose that they would slip off Kayla's wrist. He turned again to address the audience. "If the binding is too tight, you can cause circulation problems, not to mention bruising and skin chafing." The look he conveyed on the audience was stern, and Chloe knew instinctively that he was not a man who took his responsibilities lightly. "Ensuring the comfort of your sub's bindings will only serve to enhance her pleasure and your own."

Pleasure? She cast a sideways look at Xander. How soon would he expect her to indulge him in this fantasy? Would he be cross if she refused? She nibbled on her lip uncertainly. Her chest felt tight and she struggled to breathe as panic assailed her. She tried to recall their earlier discussion in the office.

Everything he had said earlier about a submissive being the one in control, the one who held the power in a D/s relationship, caused her to pause. Had he been truthful? Moreover, could she trust him? She remembered how he had made her hold tight to the bedstead the previous night, and how he had exerted his control over her body pausing in his actions until she had complied with his requests. Moisture pooled between her folds and she wriggled in her seat trying to get comfortable. Would she have felt the same excitement if he had tied her to the bed?

She wasn't sure. At the time, she had enjoyed his mastery of her mind and her body. She had complied with his wishes, but it had felt more like an erotic game they were playing than a serious issue. She cast her eye over the girl tied to the bed on the stage. That was definitely serious.

She'd loved having Xander take charge, she'd had the strongest orgasm of her life, but if he wanted more... if he wanted to tie her up... gag her.... She didn't know if she could take things that far, give up her control and let him control her altogether. She would be unable to defend herself if he turned violent, as Nick had done in the past. Doubts about agreeing to be his mistress surfaced. She wondered if it was too late to cancel the agreement she had signed earlier.

In one quick motion, Xander lifted her from the seat and placed her on his lap. "Stop wriggling!" The feel of his hard thighs beneath her bottom made her want to wriggle more and she struggled to contain her moan of arousal as he pulled her back to rest against his chest.

The demonstration on the stage had now progressed to the bed. Master Damien with the assistance of Sabrina proceeded to secure Kayla to the bed in a spread-eagle position. The rings attached to her cuffs were threaded through quick release catches built into the bed frame. He ascertained that Kayla was comfortable before he turned back to his audience.

"As you can now see, Kayla is securely and safely fastened." He continued with a warning, "Under no circumstances must you leave the room unless you have some other means of observing your partner. Your partner's safety is now in your hands and it is your duty to provide her with the utmost care."

Murmurs of assent reverberated throughout the gathered audience and Chloe was surprised at how grim Damien sounded. He obviously took his role as lecturer very seriously.

"Restraint, in the case of a submissive, can act like an aphrodisiac. Many subs will become aroused by the act of restraint alone." Damien grinned. "Now is the time to give her the pleasure she so rightly deserves."

Damien returned to the side of the bed. "The most basic of cuffs can be used in a variety of ways." He unfastened one of Kayla's ankles from the bed frame. He then proceeded to bend her knee back and across her body. He quickly threaded some rope through the ring on her ankle cuff, wrapped it behind her knee and fastened it to the cuff on her wrist. When he had finished Kayla was positioned on one side with her knee up high towards her chest. "As you will see, in this position Kayla is fully open and ready to be pleasured."

Chloe was taken aback and felt slightly nervous. She wondered if everyone that indulged in the BDSM lifestyle was an exhibitionist. The girl on the bed was wearing a short dress, but in her present position, the dress had ridden up to her waist. She wore no underwear and was fully exposed to the audience. Her arousal was clear for all to see in the gleaming folds of her sex. Chloe struggled to understand how the girl could become so aroused when surrounded by strangers. Kayla seemed to think nothing of baring all, for all to see. She could not imagine herself doing that, well, not in public. The thought of Xander having access to all of her, in private, was a different matter entirely. The irrefutable proof of her arousal caused Chloe to question how it was possible, and she turned to ask Xander for an explanation. She could not stop herself blushing when she realized he was watching her and not looking at the stage. He flashed a wide grin as he pointed towards the stage, "Eyes front, sweetheart," he instructed, his voice slightly husky, "you don't want to miss the show."

The sound of his husky tones sent her excitement higher. His words, so similar to the words he had used when they had made love and he had exerted his control over her body and mind, set off an insistent throb between her legs. From the tone of his voice, it was clear he was feeling aroused and that the act of restraining a partner turned him on. She tried to imagine herself in the other girl's position. How would she feel if she were trussed up and fully exposed to Xander's touch? Ripples of excitement spread throughout her body and she closed her eyes briefly as she tried to dispel the thought.

Damien's strong voice carried across the auditorium as he continued with his lecture. "There are of course lots of different types of restraint, as well as different types of apparatus to which you can fasten your willing partner. The St Andrew's Cross is a popular piece of kit but is more often used for restraint when flogging or using a crop."

Flogging! Did he just say flogging? Her stomach plummeted and icy fear crawled up her back. She had to have heard him wrong. "Did he say 'flogging' or did I mishear?" She asked in a whisper.

Xander put his arm around her and pulled her closer to him. "He did, but don't worry about it." He placed a light kiss on the side of her neck. "I have no intention of flogging you."

He tried to pull her closer to him, but she held herself stiffly and a little away from him. From the way she held herself it was clear he needed to make her understand that the kind of flogging they had been talking about on stage was nothing like she imagined. He reminded himself that she had recently come out of an abusive relationship and he would have to tread gently, choose his words carefully, if he didn't want to frighten her.

"You've nothing to worry about, sweetheart." He kept his voice low in an effort to reassure her. "I can see the idea doesn't appeal to you."

She leaned away from him and wrapped her arms tightly around her body. She lowered her head, tucking her chin into her chest so that he was unable to see her expression. When she spoke, her voice was no more than a tremulous croak. "I can't believe it would appeal to anyone."

He felt sick with guilt. It was obvious that she was terrified and he cursed himself for being the cause of her distress. He had known it was far too early in their relationship to visit the club, but he had wanted to see her. He could feel her trembling and wanted to scoop her into his arms and rock her as he would a distressed child. He contented himself with running his hands over her back, stroking softly in an effort to calm her fears. He needed her to understand that although others enjoyed this kind of activity, she wasn't obligated to. He was never going to force her to do something she found unpleasant.

Several minutes passed in silence, as he continued to slowly stroke and caress along her back and shoulders. As if aware that there was no imminent danger, she relaxed into his touch and her trembling started to ease.

He kept his voice low, as he asked, "Do you remember earlier, when we were talking, I explained to you that the club caters to those who enjoy fetishes?" She gave an almost imperceptible nod of her head but did not turn around to look at him. "Some folk like pain and a little pain can be very erotic." He continued to run his hands softly up and down her arms, trying to soothe her as he would a nervous filly.

Her voice was no more than a puzzled whisper when she asked, "Do you like inflicting pain?"

Did he? He thought about how he felt when the stroke of his flogger caused a responsive sub to moan aloud. The sound of his partner's excitement turned him on and, he admitted to himself, he enjoyed the feeling of power. It was not a power he would ever abuse. He closed his eyes briefly, as he contemplated his answer. "Sometimes." His voice was no more than a ragged whisper, and he wondered how she would react.

She sat up straighter and shifted away from him. She drew in a deep breath, as though building up her courage, before she asked, "Do you like to beat your partners?"

How could he explain the sexual high that could be achieved with the sting of the crop, especially when applied to a sensitive area of the body? Would she understand that it wasn't for sadistic pleasure that he employed the crop, but instead to appease the masochistic craving of a partner who enjoyed the pleasure/pain experience? His own pleasure came from helping his partner reach a state of bliss, not distress.

"No, definitely not!" He kept his voice low, but firm. "You have to understand that the types of beating you are imagining, and the type of pain served up by a loving Dom, are two different things entirely. The first, much like I imagine Nick put you through, is carried out by an out of control, abusive bastard who can't control his temper." He had placed his hands atop her shoulders and gently massaged the tense muscles as he continued to talk to her in the same low, even tone. She trembled at the mention of her ex and he struggled to keep his temper under control. "I won't lie to you, Chloe. Occasionally I like to use a flogger or a crop, but purely to bring pleasure. And only," he emphasized keen to get his point across, "with the express agreement of the recipient. Anything else would be abuse."

"Why? Why would you want to hurt someone you supposedly care for?" She sounded hurt and confused. "I don't understand you."

"I think it's more that you don't understand that there are different types of pain." She cast him a look of disbelief. "At this moment you can't envision pain as pleasurable." He took a deep breath as he thought about how to explain the pleasurable side of pain. "Okay, think about this. If I bite your neck in the heat of the moment, would you class the pain as pleasure or abuse? Would you enjoy it?" She gave an almost imperceptible nod. "If I scrape my teeth around your nipples, or if I pinch them until you feel the pull deep down in your womb, would you class that as abusive?"

She shook her head, slowly. "Well, no…." She twisted to look directly at him. "But, that's entirely different from what we were talking about."

He gave her a warm smile, glad that she was now facing him once again. "No, it's not, sweetheart. That is exactly what we were talking about; the excitement and pleasure that comes from a touch of pain. I only want what is best for you." His tone was firm, "I want to make you happy."

"And you think beating me with a whip, riding crop or whatever will make me happy?" She sounded incredulous.

"Look at me." He placed a finger gently under her chin and raised her head so that she was looking directly at him. "A little pain can be achingly sweet and erotic." At her outraged gasp, he continued, "You loved it when I pinched your nipples." He cupped her breasts and stroked across her nipples with the pads of his thumbs." He noted with pleasure that even with the lightest of touch, her nipples were starting to blossom under his fingers. She moaned softly and threw her head back, forcing her breasts more firmly into his palms. He pinched her nipples through the thin fabric of her dress, and her thighs clenched tight against his own.

"There's no use denying it… I can feel how much you enjoyed that little bit of pain." She was flushed with arousal as she looked at him. She appeared confused, but no longer afraid, and for that, he was grateful.

"Now do you understand when I say a little pain can be erotic? I'm not talking about a major beating, leaving bruises or causing harm. Pain is a tool, a way of heightening the senses, of making you more aware of your body and mine." She nibbled on her lip, bur he could see she was giving some thought to what he had explained and he was happy to leave it there. For now.

"Have your previous partner's allowed you to flog them?" she asked quietly.

He knew she wouldn't like his answer, but he refused to lie to make her feel better. "One or two," he was brutally honest. "But then again, they enjoyed it."

"I wouldn't let you flog me!" She said forlornly.

The sadness in her tone caused his gut to clench. It was as if she thought she was denying him a treat, and felt guilty that she was refusing him. It was obvious that although he may have allayed her fears somewhat, he hadn't yet convinced her that she was safe.

"Chloe, I just said I had no intention of flogging you."

He wondered if she would be surprised that he was actually pleased that she had had the courage to deny him what she thought he craved. He was glad she felt strong enough and safe enough with him to voice her fears. The last thing that he wanted was for her to be frightened of him, or to agree to something that she wasn't comfortable with, just to please him.

He lifted her from his lap and repositioned her so that she faced him. Firmly placed astride his legs she had no option but to place her hands on his shoulders to balance herself. His gaze was razor sharp as he surveyed her features.

"Xander!" She exclaimed. "How am I meant to watch the demo with my back to the stage?"

She hadn't looked at the stage in the last ten minutes, not since the subject of flogging had been mentioned. He doubted she had heard anything other than his words as they had discussed her fear. He was sure she wasn't bothered about watching the rest of the show. However, he could easily imagine her wanting to avoid his scrutiny. Not a chance. He needed to be able to see her features in order to work out what she was really feeling. Up until the point when Damien had mentioned the flogger, she had seemed to be enjoying herself.

"Forget the stage, Chloe." His tone brooked no argument, "This is more important. Tell me what you're feeling. What you're thinking."

"What?" Her eyes widened. He knew instinctively that he had caught her unaware, and he wondered how long it had been since anyone had shown real consideration for her feelings. The thought that she may have been emotionally neglected, as well as physically abused, made him angry. It also made him wonder why, when he barely knew her, he cared so much.

"You heard. Talk to me. Tell me how you feel." He leaned forward and kissed her gently. "How can I help if you won't tell me what you're afraid of? Explain to me why you are upset." He placed his arms around her waist and his hands caressed the base of her spine in slow circular motions, as he tried to calm her. "I would have sworn you were enjoying the show up until Damien mentioned the St Andrew's Cross."

Chloe smiled tremulously at him, maybe hoping to put off the discussion he was intent on having with her.

"I'm cross, not upset."

His stomach sank at her blatant lie. How long was it going to take her to open up and trust him he wondered? "And now, you've just lied to me." He shook his head. "I know you're upset. I can feel it in the way you tremble. I can hear it in your voice." Sadly, he added, "I can still see traces of fear in your eyes."

He gave her a smile of encouragement. "Talk to me, sweetheart. You have no need to be afraid of me. I will never deliberately hurt you." He gave a cynical laugh. "I won't bite." He brought a hand up her back to cup her nape as he slowly moved her closer to him. "On second thought, maybe I will." He dipped his head and playfully laved at the side of her neck as his hand held her in position.

He knew he wasn't playing fair as he showered her throat with small nips and kisses, but he needed to move her into a more receptive frame of mind.

"Xander. No!" She forced her head back and out of his reach. "I need to think. I can't think when you do that."

He threw her a wicked grin, unable to hide the fact that her admission had pleased him. Nevertheless, he wasn't going to be so easily sidetracked.

"So answer my question. Don't think too much about it, just open up and tell me what you're thinking." He stroked the side of her face with his thumb and hoped she would be tempted enough to turn into his caress, but he wasn't really surprised when she resisted. Her guard was up. His gaze was steady as he held her gaze. "I promise, Chloe. There is nothing you can say that will shock me, or make me cross with you.

Well, apart from lying that is. For a relationship like ours to work both partners, have to be truthful. I need to be able to trust what you say. "

She chewed nervously on her lip, as she looked him over. She cast a quick glance toward the door at the rear, and he wondered if she was intending to run away from him again. Tension gnawed at his stomach and he fought down his impatience as he struggled to remain silent. Uncertainty drew her delicate brows together and he watched as a range of emotions flitted across her face. He needed to allow her time to digest his words and compose her thoughts without influence from him. The decision to stay with him had to be her own.

After a long pause, during which time he had continued to stroke her arms, she finally said, "I don't like the idea of being beaten, flogged or whatever else you want to call it." She sat up straighter and looked him straight in the eye. "I've been down that road before, and never again. Not for you, not for anyone..." She tailed off as though her spurt of courage had suddenly deserted her.

"Well said, sweetheart!" He congratulated her for having the courage to open up and say exactly what was on her mind. "And what makes you think I am going to beat you?" The idea was like a sucker punch to his gut. It was no surprise to him, given her past relationship, that she would feel this way. However, he was disappointed that she still appeared to view some forms of BDSM play as abusive. He couldn't think about that now. He had to concentrate on making her feel better, making sure she understood she was safe with him.

"How do I know if you will or you won't?" The look on her face was decidedly wary. "I never in a million years thought Nick would hit me." A look of shame flashed across her features, and she hid her face in her hands. Full of pity, he watched as she struggled to control her emotions. A moment or two was all she took, before she swiped her eyes with shaky fingers and said sadly. "I loved him, I thought he loved me."

"I'm not Nick!" He kept his voice low, even though he hated being compared to that bastard.

"No, you're not. However, I knew him for a hell of a lot longer than I've known you, and I would never have believed it if someone had told me he was an abuser." She shrugged her shoulders. "Maybe I'm just not a very good judge of character," she said bitterly with a ring of disgust. He saw her shame and realized that she no longer trusted herself to make the right decisions. She waved a hand behind her back, indicating the stage. "He was talking about a cross and flogging.... How am I supposed to know what you're going to do when we're alone?"

"Simple, all you have to do is ask." He reached out and squeezed her hands gently. "I will never lie to you Chloe. You may not like what I have to say sometimes, but you can rest assured it will be the truth."

The look she gave him was skeptical. He knew exactly how violent her relationship with Nick had been. He had read the medical report. He wondered how she must have felt having to face each day with fear and dread. He realized she would need support to learn to trust her own judgment about other people. He vowed to help her overcome her fears. He would teach her to trust him; they just needed more time together to build that trust.

"Well then," she appeared to gather her courage and looked him straight in the eye, her muscles quivering with tension as she asked, "Are you expecting me to submit to a flogging?"

He could see her holding her breath as she awaited his reply. She delighted him with her courage, and he wanted to congratulate her on standing up for herself, but he didn't think she would appreciate his timing.

"Not if you don't want to," he replied firmly.

"Well, I don't! I definitely do not want to be flogged," she reiterated softly.

"We'll make that a hard limit then." He held her gaze. "Any other hard limits I should know about?"

She looked puzzled and he had to remind himself that she probably had no idea what he meant.

He cupped her face as he watched her intently. "In our lifestyle, Chloe, it is normal to negotiate a sexual encounter beforehand. Hard and soft limits are agreed upon, along with a chosen safe word. Many couples will draw up a contract. It is legally binding and to go against someone's limits is classed as assault."

Her eyes were so expressive and they opened wide as she stared at him. He wanted to laugh when she asked, "Contract, as in the type of contract we just signed?" He could see her mentally backtracking over the contract she had signed, probably worrying over what she had agreed to.

He could contain his amusement no longer and smiled. "No. Nothing like the contract we signed earlier." He shook his head at her misunderstanding; before he went on to explain. "That was a mere formality, a legal protecting of privacy for us both. A BDSM contract is a different thing altogether and not something we are anywhere near ready to enter into."

She gave him a rueful smile and he felt at last that the tension between them was beginning to ease. "Well, what kind of contract is it?" She sounded confused but looked a little excited as she awaited his answer.

"Well, sweetheart," he leaned closer and whispered conspiratorially in her ear, "you could call it a sexual contract. We would sit down and talk about what you do or don't like, what you are willing to experiment with and what you want to avoid." She stayed silent as he continued, "A soft limit would be something you might like to try, but is always renegotiable. A hard limit is something you will not try under any circumstance. So for instance, we now know that flogging is on your hard limit list. Therefore… no flogging in our playroom."

She looked dazed. "Are you telling me that people actually sit down and agree how they will make love, before the event? It doesn't seem very spontaneous or exciting."

He laughed aloud. "You think not?" He was amused at her naivety and was looking forward to introducing her to the pleasures to come. "Our sex life will be a bit more than vanilla, so we will put safeguards in place. Some people enjoy their sex play a little edgier than others do. It's wise to agree beforehand exactly what your limits are."

"And that's what we'll do?" She leaned in closer to his chest and he was pleased to note that her body didn't feel as tense as it had earlier. She blushed lightly as she continued, "You want us to sit down and discuss our sexual likes and dislikes before we go to bed again?"

Not likely, he couldn't wait that long to be buried inside her again. "It's what we'll do before I introduce you to my playroom." At her quizzical look, he grinned and quantified his statement, "My personal BDSM room. Playroom is the usual name for a room at home."

"Oh, my." She sounded shocked. "You actually have a separate room just for that. At home!"

Her tone may have been shocked, but he could see the excitement simmering in her eyes and knew she was tempted to explore his lifestyle further. The thought made him hard and he wondered how long he would have to wait before she was ready.

"It's there, ready and waiting whenever you feel ready." His stomach muscles clenched in anticipation. He closed his eyes, giving thanks that the crisis appeared to have now passed. The tension between them had eased and she no longer looked like she was going to bolt from him. Relief swept over him and he was keen to get back to their discussion. "Now, sweetheart. No changing the subject this time." He pulled her closer, enjoying the feel of her against his chest. "Did you see anything in tonight's show that you enjoyed?"

"Such as?" The look she gave him was coy.

When he arched a brow at her query, she cast her lashes down across her eyes and refused to meet his gaze. He was bemused at her apparent embarrassment. How could she be so shy when he already knew every inch of her? He took pity on her, as she was obviously unused to talking about her sexual feelings, and decided to help her out.

He cupped her chin and lifted her head up for his kiss. "What did you think of Kayla's leather cuffs?"

Her tongue swiped across her bottom lip and she shielded her eyes with her lashes as she replied, "They were alright I suppose if you're into that kind of thing."

"Eyes on me, sweetheart." Her eyes shot open and she looked directly into his gaze. He watched her pupils dilate and knew that she was remembering the last time he had used those words. "Do you think it's the kind of thing you could be into?" God, he hoped so. He would love to see her cuffed and tied to his bed.

"I'm.... I'm not sure." She sounded uncertain, but she was slightly breathless and he went with his hunch. "How about we put that down as a soft limit?"

Chapter Nine

Chloe was in a daze as she snuggled against Xander in the back of the car. Xander had called the night to a halt and they were now on their way back to London. It was late and she felt very tired. Although he had encouraged her to nap on the return journey, she was unable to sleep.

She kept thinking of all the things she had seen, and the things they had discussed. She closed her eyes and feigned sleep, hoping to have some time to gather her thoughts together before they arrived at her hotel.

She wondered if she had made a mistake in agreeing to become his mistress. The idea had never sat easy with her, but she was in a bind and it had seemed like a reasonable solution at the time. It wasn't that Xander was unattractive or that she was not attracted. It was quite the opposite. The chemistry between them was explosive and she was grateful she was going to have the chance to spend more time with him. Nevertheless, she hadn't reckoned on him having a kinky side. His previous partners had apparently been happy to indulge his dominant personality, but she wasn't sure that she could.

Although he had promised he would never hurt her physically, his lifestyle seemed to embrace pain. She understood that a little pain was erotic, however, how much did he consider a little? When he pulled sharply on her nipples or nipped her neck with his teeth, she had felt more excitement than pain. When he had pinched the bud between her legs, her orgasm had crashed over her. However, she had the feeling he was going to need more. He wanted to bind her. What would he do to her when she was bound and helpless? What if she panicked and couldn't go through with it? Her excitement started to build, and then crashed as she wondered if she would be able to satisfy him or if he would quickly become bored with her.

The contract she had signed was for twelve months, which now didn't seem very long. If she gave herself up to his care for the next year, what would she do when the contract expired? After only a couple of days, she was already relying on him to keep her safe and the future without him seemed bleak.

She trembled in nervous anticipation as she recalled his comments about Kayla's cuffs. She would never have believed that the idea of being restrained would have appealed to her, but now, the thought of being restrained by him, caused her body to weep. She had already felt the force of his dominance when he had insisted she hold onto the bedstead and had to admit that she had found the experience stimulating. She swept her tongue across her suddenly dry lips. She couldn't help wondering how much more stimulating it would have been if she had actually been bound.

As if he had guessed that she wasn't asleep, he pulled her more tightly against him.

"What's going through that head of yours, sweetheart? I can almost hear the cogs ticking."

She was startled and her eyes shot open as his face loomed over her. She blurted out the first thing that came into her head. "Where's the fun in being tied up? I wouldn't be able to touch you."

His eyes widened and his eyebrows rose. She could see he was surprised at her question and she wondered if he was pleased that she had been thinking about their earlier conversation.

Xander took a deep breath, breathing in the scent of her perfume and her arousal. Her question had taken him by surprise and he gave some thought to her query. He liked the thought of her wanting to touch him and his hands itched to touch her, but he restrained himself. Now was the time to get to know her and understand better what she needed from him.

"But, I would be able to touch you." He gave her a wide grin. "Imagine the anticipation and the pleasure you would receive if I had access to all of you. Imagine how many times I would be able to bring you to the brink before I took you over the edge."

He kept his voice low as he whispered in her ear. "Close your eyes and think about being tied naked on my bed."

She closed her eyes as he continued, "I'd have access to every part of you. I could start at your feet and work my way up." She trembled slightly in his arms. "I'd shower you with feather-light kisses, up every inch of your legs until I reached my goal."

He trailed his fingers along the length of her arms. When he reached her neck, he cupped her jaw and lifted her face to his own. She opened her eyes and looked directly at him. "When I reached your core, I would spread you with my tongue and sip the nectar you had produced for me alone. I would take great delight in seeing your body dance."

She clenched her thighs together and closed her eyes once again when he cupped her mound through the confines of her clothing.

"After I had my fill, I would work my way up to your glorious breasts." His hands slowly trailed up and over her stomach until he held a breast in each hand. He brushed the pads of his thumbs across her nipples, which had perked and were protruding through the fabric of her dress. "I could feast on these berries and never feel hungry." He pinched her nipples softly and she gave a soft moan. He couldn't contain his own need filled groan.

"After a bit of training," his voice turned ragged, "I would be able to make you come without even touching you." He pinched her nipples lightly and she arched her back forcing her breasts nearer to him. "You would learn to come on command."

"Imagine the strength of your orgasm when it finally peaks. I can promise, it will be like nothing you have felt before."

Xander watched as she opened her eyes and struggled to swallow, before she asked, "I get all that just for being tied up?" She was watching him closely.

"No. You get all that because you trust me enough to submit." He gave her a slow smile. "Because you will have given me the responsibility for your pleasure and will have shown that you trust me to take care of you."

She tilted her head to one side as she asked quizzically, "And what do you get out of it?"

"I get my pleasure knowing that you have received yours." He gave her a wolfish grin.

"And that's enough for you?" Her tone was husky with arousal and his cock twitched as he wondered how wet she was.

"More than!" He stated firmly. They still had a way to go before they reached their destination, and he could wait no longer to feel her warmth wrapped around him. "Let me show you." He spanned her waist with his hands and lifted her onto his lap. "Open your legs and straddle me," he commanded. He positioned her so that she faced the front of the car and had her back resting against his chest. He cupped her jaw and settled her head into the crook of his neck. "Stay still."

Her breathing was erratic and he wondered whether that was due to excitement or trepidation. He received his answer when his palms skimmed lightly across her chest and she moaned low in the back of her throat. His excitement spiked and his cock rose painfully under her backside.

He wrapped his arms around her middle, holding her close as he whispered in her ear. "Now we're going to play a little game." She trembled within his embrace, and he continued, "I'm going to give you a taste of the pleasures to come."

She stiffened in his arms. "What! Now?" She whispered fiercely. "What about the driver?" He couldn't see her clearly within the dark confines of the car, but he could feel her flush against his skin. He reminded himself again that she was inexperienced in the games he liked to play and that he would have to go slowly. He needed her cooperation if he was going to make this a good experience for her.

"Relax. For this time only I'll put up the privacy screen. He won't be able to see a thing." He leaned forward and pressed a button on the center console and a screen rose to block off her view of the driver and the distance ahead.

"Now relax. Enjoy."

She relaxed slightly in his hold, but he could still feel the unbridled tension throughout her body. He cupped her jaw with one hand and brought her face up to his. He removed the pins from her hair and let it fall to tumble around her shoulders.

"I like it down." He proceeded to weave his fingers through her hair and he gave her no chance to reply before he tugged on her hair and pulled her head back exposing her throat. Turning her face upward, he curled his body around her and planted a line of tender kisses along her jaw before his mouth sought hers. He kissed her with precision, starting tender and slow, and was rewarded with the murmur of appreciation she moaned softly into his mouth.

Her soft moan drove him on. He pulled her closer and began a thorough exploration of her mouth. He licked along the seam of her lips, before plunging his tongue inside to stroke and caress wherever he could reach. She reached up with her hands to pull him closer and pressed herself firmly against his chest. Her tongue matched his, stroke for stroke, and her breathing became no more than a series of breathless sighs. She was driving him mad. He had never felt so out of control and he struggled to regain his composure. He had promised her a lesson in pleasure and he didn't want to disappoint. He also needed to know if she would submit to him.

He brought their kiss to halt, slowly, winding down with teasing kisses along the line of her jaw. He was back in control. He released her from the cage of his arms. The need for her submission drove him and his body remained tense as he issued his first command. "Stand up and remove your panties."

Her audible gasp reverberated through him and he wondered if she would obey. "Now!" His tone was sharper than he intended, but he was pleasantly surprised when she slipped from his lap and shimmied the panties down the length of her legs.

He patted his knee and warmly invited, "Back on my lap, sweetheart."

She had kept her back to him as she removed the slip of silk and lace, and she retook her position on his lap without saying a word. He could feel her body trembling and hoped it was because she was excited. She still grasped her panties tightly in a clenched hand. He removed the damp panties from her grasp, bringing them to his face to inhale deeply of her arousal. "My favorite scent." He put them in his pocket. "I may or may not give them back to you."

He placed an arm around her waist. "Relax." He drew her back, once again settling her head against his shoulder. "This little game is all about making you feel good."

He opened his legs, causing hers to spread. He trailed his fingers up her legs, caressing in slow circles over her silk clad thighs. Her body started to tremble and she gave a small gasp when he reached her stocking tops. "Sshh… I'm going to make you feel so good," he promised softly in her ear.

Her flesh quivered when he stroked his fingers along her bare skin, nearer and nearer to the heart of her. As he teased the flesh of her inner thighs, she moaned in need and wriggled her body against him.

She grasped his forearms tightly as if she was trying to direct his movements. He stilled his fingers against her inner thighs.

"Put your hands up and around the back of my neck." He was surprised at the hoarseness of his own voice. She had gotten to him more than he had thought possible.

"Mmm.... What?" She seemed disorientated.

"Hands up behind my head," he repeated. She didn't move.

"Now!" He commanded firmly, "or we stop playing."

She released her hold on his arms and raised her arms to place her hands behind his head. The position caused her body to arch and thrust her breasts high and close to his face. He licked his lips in anticipation, but first, he had other pleasures to bestow.

"Keep your arms there and your reward will be sweet," he promised in her ear, as his fingers once again continued their path towards her core.

When his fingers reached their goal, he swallowed hard, as he realized that she was more than ready for him. The tops of her thighs were coated with her own juices and the heat from her core had him biting his lip in an effort to stifle his groan. She was going to be the death of him. He had set out to pleasure her, but the pleasure so far was all his.

He parted her labia and thrust a couple of fingers straight into her. She gasped loudly and clenched her muscles around him. His fingers slipped in with ease as she was so swollen, wet and ready for him. He stroked her clit with his thumb and she jerked on his lap. Her breathing became more and more ragged as he teased her.

With each stroke against her clit, she moaned louder and her body undulated against his, creating a delicious friction. His erection pressed painfully against the confines of his pants and he knew he couldn't hold on much longer. He took a deep breath as he fought to bring his body back under control.

He skimmed his hands up her body, pulling up her short dress until is was bunched above her waist. He undid the fastening of the halter and dragged the top down to expose her breasts, and her ruby nipples, which now stood proud. With one hand, he teased and tweaked her nipples while the other returned to stroke between her legs. When her breathing became no more than a ragged gasp and her legs started to twitch, he ceased to stroke her.

"Xander, please..."

"Please? Please what?" The effort to maintain his control kept his tone hard. "Tell me exactly what you want." He needed to hear her vocalize her need.

"I want... I need... you to finish what you started," she said brokenly.

"Like this?" He ran his thumb in circles around her tightly erect clit. "Is this what you want sweetheart?"

"Oh, God. Yes." As much as she was able to, supported on his lap as she was, she lifted her mound up to meet his hand.

"And this." He pinched an erect nipple between his fingers and she moaned aloud.

He plunged a couple of fingers inside her and her body grasped them greedily. He could feel her inner muscles pulse as her juices coated his hand. He needed to be inside her, but more than that, he needed her to beg for his possession.

He withdrew his fingers, covered in her cream and trailed a slick path up her body. He circled her nipple with the moisture before he bent his head to lave and suck up her essence. He smeared the remnants across her lips. "Open and suck."

In the dim glow cast by the highway lights, he watched as she curled the tip of her tongue around his finger, licking every bit of it clean. His cock pulsed as he imagined the havoc her tongue would cause on his body. She moaned when he withdrew his finger and her eyes dilated with arousal. He noted with pleasure that she still held her arms in position. Maybe, he thought, she wouldn't take as long to train as he had thought.

He curled an arm around her middle and hugged her; before he let his head loll back against the headrest. He wondered how she would react to the ceasing of all activity. He had deliberately left her near her peak. He wanted to hear her demand the satisfaction he had promised. He needed to know that she could vocalize her desires, otherwise her training was going to take longer than he had envisioned. He couldn't look at her, without wanting her, so he closed his eyes as he awaited her response.

"Xander." She sounded cross and a little confused. He battled to keep the smile from his face.

"Mmm…" he murmured quietly, "Did you want something?"

He heard her gasp of indignation or was it anger? He opened one eye slowly to observe her. She had been so close to cumming several times, yet each time he had called a halt, preventing her from reaching her peak. He knew she had to feel frustrated, and possibly cheated out of the joy he had told her he would deliver but would she ask him to ease the ache? It was his intention to use her frustration as a tool, as a form of training. He wanted her to open up and talk to him about her wants and needs. He wanted her to understand how important open communication would be when they were negotiating a scene.

She shimmied off his lap to sit on the adjoining seat. She turned away from him, her hands clenched tightly in her lap. He placed his hands on her shoulders and gently massaged her tense muscles for a moment or two. When he tried to turn her around, she shrugged his hands away.

"Don't touch me!" She sounded like she was crying and his stomach plunged. That wasn't the response he had expected.

He patted the middle of her back, much as one would do with a child, as he attempted to comfort her. He had expected her to be cross, maybe to shout at him and accuse him of being a tease, thereby opening up a discussion on her needs and desires. He hadn't expected her to break down in tears.

Keeping his voice low, he asked, "Are you going to tell me why you're crying?"

"As if you didn't know." She sighed wearily, before snapping, "Have I got 'gullible' stamped across my forehead?"

"What?" He was taken aback. What the hell? It was beginning to look like his plan had seriously backfired. "What exactly does that mean?" He asked quietly.

"It means," she spun around to face him, "that I am sick to death of men who take their pleasure and leave their partner wanting! To think I listened to all your promises and it turns out you're nothing more than a selfish bastard, like all the rest."

His angel had suddenly found her voice and he was in real trouble. Nevertheless, he couldn't help but point out, "I've not been satisfied either, sweetheart." He kept his tone low but firm. "You are not the only one feeling frustrated." The ache to possess her was burning a hole in his gut.

"I'm not the one that called a halt." The look in her eye was positively cold.

She had him there. He thought about what she had said with regard to selfish partners and realized what he should have guessed at the outset. She'd given him enough hints. Nick had not paid much attention to her needs, and he wondered how many times she had been left disappointed. It was no wonder she'd been hesitant to talk about what she wanted. His stomach churned with guilt as he realized that by pushing her to voice her desires, he had brought bad memories to the fore. He'd unwittingly hurt her and he made up his mind that she definitely wouldn't be left wanting tonight. It was up to him to ensure she received as much pleasure as her body could take.

"Tell me what you want, sweetheart," he encouraged.

"You know what I want." She sounded belligerent and not at all submissive. He would have to change that.

"You still want to cum?" He queried, knowing he was being a bastard.

"What do you think?" Her eyes blazed with indignation, and he wanted to gather her in his arms and erase the previous wrongs inflicted upon her.

"I think," he said slowly, as he watched her intently, "that your body is crying out for release."

She refused to meet his eye. "Maybe it is, maybe it isn't," she murmured.

"I can give you that release if you'll let me." He stroked his fingers down the length of her arms. "I will make you feel so good, you'll be on a high for a week." He wasn't bragging. He knew that given the chance, he could have her writhing in ecstasy. "Now stop prevaricating and answer my question." His tone was unyielding. "Do you still want to cum?"

"Of course I do!" She wailed.

"Then tell me what you want." His tone was harsh, but he was determined that he would get her to talk.

She was looking at him as though he had gone mad. Her mouth was pinched as she tipped her head to one side and looked him over.

"What do you want from me?" She looked confused and he reminded himself that he needed to go slowly with her. He grasped her hands and held them gently within his own. He stroked his thumbs across the pulse points on her wrists. "I want to give you pleasure." He looked directly into her eyes. "I want you screaming my name when you cum."

Her eyes flared and he knew he had her. "Well, that's not going to happen now." She sounded unforgiving as she tried to pull her hands free. He tightened his grasp.

"Why not?"

"Because.... Because.... I'm no longer in the mood to indulge you." She looked at him mutinously. His kitten had turned into a tiger and the venom in her voice excited him. His cock twitched. He looked forward to channeling her passion in another direction.

"Ah, but sweetheart, I am in the mood to indulge you." He winked and patted his knee, silently inviting her to climb back onto his lap.

"Just like that!" She looked at him through half-closed lashes. "You expect me to get back on your lap as if nothing has happened?"

"I do," he said firmly. "If you want me to ease the sweet ache you're feeling." He looked at her pointedly. "If you want to be my sub."

Her jaw dropped and her lips formed an O though she uttered not a sound. He felt his own heart rate increase as he waited to see what she would do. His stomach muscles clenched as the seconds stretched and he allowed her time to think about what he had just said.

Her face was a picture of indecision. He read the various thoughts that flashed across her face. At first, she looked angry, then skeptical. She looked at his lap and he saw longing and a flicker of desire, but she made no move towards him. She needed encouragement.

"Now," he said firmly as he patted his knee once more. "I'm waiting."

Chloe wasn't sure what she wanted. She looked from his lap to his face. His features were harsh and the telltale beat at the side of his jaw betrayed his tension. She was angry and disappointed, but her body still clamored for release. She thought about the pleasure he had promised her and her internal muscles clenched with need. She may not have made up her mind, but her body knew what it wanted. He'd promised her release, and deep down she knew he was a man of his word. She considered the concept of becoming his sub and wondered if she was ready for such a step. The thought of being on the receiving end of his undivided attention caused her body to weep.

"Be brave," he smiled at her encouragingly. "I'm not going to hurt you. I want to make you feel good."

She took a deep breath and hoped she hadn't made the wrong decision. She wriggled onto his lap.

"Good girl." His words were no more than a breathy whisper against her ear, but they caused a warm glow to unfurl inside her. She wanted to be his girl, she wanted to please him. When he tugged her back against his chest she allowed herself to relax there.

She watched as his hands came to rest upon her thighs where he grasped the hem of her dress. She trembled as he peeled the dress up and away from her body, and wondered if she was brave enough to do whatever he asked. Could she trust him enough to let go of her inhibitions? He discarded her dress on the seat opposite with a flick of his wrist.

"You're beautiful." He sounded sincere and she was delighted that she pleased him. She cast a quick eye over the privacy screen and prayed the driver could not see her on his lap wearing nothing but hold-ups and high heels.

As if he had noticed the direction of her gaze, he embraced her tightly in his arms. "Relax. Don't think about anything but us." He sounded so confident and sure of his ability. She found herself wondering if he could really make her feel more than she already had. Surely, she thought, it couldn't get any better. Her thoughts brought a blush that suffused her body, drenching her in heat.

She closed her eyes, blocking out everything but sensation as he slowly skimmed his hands down her body to the apex of her thighs. She had kept her legs closed when she sat upon his lap, and his hands insinuated themselves between her thighs. He exerted a light pressure on her inner thighs and she understood, without instruction, that he wished her to open her legs.

She parted her legs, craving his touch at her core. "Wider, sweetheart." His tone was husky with arousal. "Straddle my legs and raise your arms and put them behind my head. Hold on tight. Do not let go or we will stop again."

She inhaled, taking a deep breath to steady her nerves as she wondered what he would ask next. Would she be able to meet his demands?

Her head rested in the crook of his neck and she could hear his heartbeat, strong and steady. She realized that although he had disappointed her, he still made her feel safe and she made up her mind to trust him, to let him guide her.

"Now, darling," he whispered in her ear, "we'll see about easing your frustration."

Her sex clenched at the promise in his voice and every muscle in her body felt tight with tension. "And yours too I hope?" Surely, he wasn't go to see to her pleasure and neglect his own.

"Don't worry about me. This is all about you. What you want and what you need." He sounded so calm whereas she felt like she was teetering on the edge of a precipice. How did he do that?

His fingers stroked nearer and nearer to her core and her excitement grew. The anticipation of his touch had her tilting her hips, trying to bring his fingers closer. "Naughty!" He chuckled softly. "The point of this game, Chloe, is to teach control. You have to learn to control your instincts, and more importantly," he grazed the side of her neck with his teeth, "you have to learn to let me take control."

"You are in control." Frustration was making her cranky.

"And don't you forget it." He replied firmly. "So be good, let me take care of you. Trust me to know what you need."

"Yes, Master." She had meant her quip to be sarcastic, but she realized that he misinterpreted her response, when he groaned softly and replied, "Exactly. From this moment on I will be your Master and you will learn to heed my commands."

Master. Master. He is my Master. The words spun around in her head as she questioned why her body trembled at the tone of his voice. He sounded so forceful, yet not in a violent way. His self-assurance had her quivering inside as she speculated on whether or not she could obey him. She had been controlled by Nick. Until tonight, she'd been firm in her own mind, that she would never let anyone control her again. However, this felt different. With Nick, the control had been taken away, without her agreement. Xander, on the other hand, was asking her to give him control.

"Where were we?" He teased as his fingers reached her core. He parted her labia and stroked slowly between her folds. He stroked nearer and nearer to her clit, but didn't touch it. She wanted to scream in frustration and could not hold back her muttered plea. "Please…."

"Tell me what you want." His breathing sounded harsh against her neck.

Christ, was the man thick? He was driving her mad with need, stoking her fire but refusing to take her any higher. She didn't think she would be able to bear it if he left her hanging again.

She tried to control her breathing as she panted, "Isn't it obvious?"

"Perfectly."

She was puzzled. What the hell was he asking for if he already knew the answer? "Then why ask?"

"Simple. You need to learn to tell me what you do or don't like. I want to hear you tell me what you want."

She felt awkward. She wasn't used to talking about the sex act and yet he seemed to expect it. "Just keep doing what you were doing," she muttered.

"Like this?" His fingers trailed slickly through her swollen folds and he stroked her sensitized flesh. Not once did he touch her clit and her frustration mounted. She sucked in her stomach muscles as she fought for strength, but she was unable to tell him what she wanted.

"Is that okay?" He sounded like he was laughing at her.

She clenched her teeth in an effort to prevent herself screaming at him, but could not prevent the soft groan of despair rushing from her throat. She shook her head. "No, I need more!"

"Like this?" He inserted two fingers inside her and her body clenched around him, but he kept his fingers still.

She wanted to bounce up and down on his fingers but managed to restrain herself. She didn't want him to think she was depraved. "More." She gasped. "Please…"

"How's this?" He stroked his fingers in and out of her body, in an agonizingly slow dance that did nothing to appease her building hunger.

"Harder. Faster." She was beyond thought and reduced to begging.

"Good, girl." He sounded pleased, but at that moment she didn't really care. She needed to reach her peak. The tension was building within and her internal muscles rippled in response to his increasingly stronger strokes into her body but it wasn't enough. She wanted to wail. She tried to reach her peak, but it was no use. She was never going to cum with finger penetration alone, she needed further stimulation.

"In a Dom/sub relationship it's important to be open and talk about your needs." Xander murmured in her ear. Why, she wondered, was he starting a conversation now? "I want to know what you like, and what you dislike." His tone hardened. "I need to know when you want more, or if you want to stop."

Her mind latched onto the word 'stop' and her breathing hitched. She would never forgive him if he stopped now. Please, please, please she prayed, don't let him call a halt now. She didn't think she would be able to bear the disappointment.

"Don't stop!" She couldn't keep the note of panic from her voice.

She cringed as she realized how desperate she must sound. "I'll not stop unless you tell me to." He sounded amused, but she was past caring. Her body was clamoring for release and she screwed her eyes tightly shut, in an effort to block out everything but the sensation he was creating. It was good, but not good enough. Why didn't he stroke her clit? She moved her hips, squirming on his lap as she tried to angle her most sensitive spot closer to his hand. Frustration had her biting her lip.

"What do you want, sweetheart?" His husky whisper against her ear was sheer torture. "Tell me what you need."

"I need more…." She tailed off. How could she tell him exactly what she wanted?

"What kind of more?" His tone was coaxing. "Tell me exactly what you want and I'll give it to you."

Her body was tense with need. She didn't understand his lifestyle, but she did understand the message in his words. If she told him what she wanted, he would deliver. She needed more stimulation to take her to her peak and she was tired of playing games. Her body couldn't take any more. "I need you to… to stroke… stroke my clit." The words tumbled out in an incoherent murmur, but she didn't doubt that he had understood her. Instantly his thumb applied pressure to her sensitive nib, and he proceeded to alternately rotate and pinch her clit.

"You only needed to ask, darling." He grazed the side of her throat with his teeth. "How does that feel?"

"Mmm…." Good. Oh so good. She couldn't begin to put her feelings into words. His fingers worked their magic and she was so close to cumming. Feeling as if she was running a marathon her breaths came in short, sharp gasps as she aimed for her release. Her legs started to twitch and she knew she couldn't hold back much longer. When he ceased all movement, just as she was about to peak, she was dumbfounded. She lowered her arms jerkily and twisted round on his lap so that she could look at him. Surely, she prayed, he didn't intend to deprive her a second time.

He lay against the leather headrest and he met her gaze straight on. He didn't look in the least bit guilty.

"Why?" Her voice came out as no more than a hoarse whisper.

"Why did I stop?" He was watching her intently. His tone serious, he continued, "I stopped because from now on in, all your pleasure belongs to me. It is up to me to decide if and when you will be satisfied."

"But… but, you promised!" She was almost beside herself with disbelief. "You said," she couldn't hold back the sob of disappointment in her voice, "that all I had to do was tell you what I wanted and you'd deliver." She felt like he had played her for a fool.

"And I will, sweetheart. Soon," he promised as he wrapped his arms around her and pulled her toward him. When she was mere inches from his lips, he continued, "I don't want you to cum until I am buried deep inside you. I want to be engulfed in your heat, coated in your cream and being squeezed by your pussy when your orgasm hits." Oh God, it sounded so good. "I want to look into your eyes when you scream my name."

Her body clenched impulsively. She recalled the first time he had made love to her and his demand that she keep her eyes open and on him. Watching her pleasure peak was obviously something he enjoyed, and who was she to deny him, when he was giving her that pleasure. She just wished he would get on with the delivery.

"Sit back a bit, darling." He put his hands around her waist and lifted her forward on his lap, before reaching down between them to undo his belt. Her mouth felt dry as she watched him lower his zip. His erect cock sprung free and she moaned aloud, aroused once more at the sight of him.

He placed his hands under her arms and lifted her closer. "Up on your knees, sweetheart." His hands moved to cup her bottom as he guided her over his erection. "Straddle me and take your pleasure."

Her legs stretched wide as she straddled his thighs and she could feel her muscles straining as she slowly lowered her body over him. She grasped his shoulders to help her balance, and threw her head back, as he filled her completely.

He hissed through gritted teeth as she enveloped him, but he didn't move. Instead, he placed his hands on either side of her hips and encouraged her to ride him. The delicious friction as he stretched her caused her muscles to vibrate around him, and she could feel every inch of him throb. Her body was still sensitive, still highly aroused and she lifted herself slowly. She gasped when he grabbed her hips and slammed her back down onto him. His eyes flared, but still he watched her. He was buried so deep in inside her, she couldn't tell where she ended and he began, and she loved being so close to him.

He rocked himself into her as he continued to control her movements. She could feel her climax start to build, slow ripples overtook her body and she closed her eyes once more. He held her still. "Eyes on me," he commanded.

He held her steady, not allowing her to move until she opened her eyes once more. His jaw was clenched and she knew he was struggling to contain his own release. Knowing the effect she was having on him, boosted her confidence and her spirits soared. She tightened her pelvic muscles around him and he uttered a low groan. He worked a hand between them and stroked her clit. "Now you can cum."

His other hand gripped her hip painfully as he guided her movements, up and down, faster and harder with each downward stroke. Her breathing became no more than breathless gasps as she struggled to keep up with the pace he had set. He was no longer being gentle, and although she was on top, he was the one in charge.

"Cum!" He pinched her clit with his fingers and tipped her over the edge. As the convulsions of her orgasm shook her body, she screamed out his name. He roared as his own release hit, and she could feel his hot seed pumping into her as she trembled in his arms.

She had never known anything like it. He continued to gently rock into her, as her body trembled around him. His slow movements seemed to extend the life of her climax and she wondered if she would ever stop shaking. She closed her eyes, wrapped herself around him and just held on. She hadn't really believed that he could make it better than ever before, but he had delivered on his promise. She had never imagined that she could feel so good. The sensations bombarding her body overwhelmed her. Euphoria hit and she felt like she was floating away from him. She felt strangely disorientated yet if this was a dream, she didn't want it to end. She clung to him taking comfort from the fact that she could feel him. His heart was racing beneath her cheek and his chest rose rhythmically as he cocooned her in his arms. She felt safe.

Enfolded in his arms she couldn't move. She was happy to stay on his lap as he stroked her back. He held her firmly against his chest. He was whispering words against her ear, his voice no more than a soft croon that seemed to come from far away. She couldn't take in what he was saying, but the tone of his voice was comforting and she snuggled closer to him. She wanted to thank him. To tell him just how wonderful she felt, but she couldn't think straight enough to form the words. His heartbeat was strong and steady, just like him. For the first time in a long time, she felt safe. She also felt incredibly confused as she wondered if her submission was what had made the difference. Was submission a state of mind?

Xander held her close as her breathing calmed. He'd whispered words of praise in her ear, telling her how much she had pleased him and how good she had made him feel. He was still on a high. Her submission had been beautiful and he couldn't believe his luck in finding her. He gathered her closer, pleased when her hands crept around his neck as she clung to him. He rocked her gently in his arms as she started to drift asleep. A surge of protectiveness washed over him and he knew he didn't want to let her go. He would make sure she was decently dressed before they left the car, but he needed to hold her a while longer. As they approached the City, he instructed the driver to drive around a while. He was enjoying the feel of her asleep in his arms and was pleased that she felt safe enough to be able to let down her guard and fall asleep on his lap. For a while at the club, he had been worried that his lifestyle was going to make her afraid of him. Now, he knew different. She was going to make a fantastic sub and he could hardly wait to take her home and make a proper start on her training.

The little scene he had just enjoyed had only whetted his appetite. She had been more responsive than he could have hoped, considering her past. Moreover, she was a quick learner. He smiled to himself as he mulled over the pleasures he had yet to introduce, and once again, his body started to stir.

As they approached the City, he knew he would have to wake her up. "Angel," he cupped her chin and raised her head; feathering light kisses across her brow and down the side of her face. "Time to wake up, sweetheart."

"No… no yet," she murmured, "let me sleep a while longer."

"If that's what you really want, sweetheart," he teased. "I don't mind carrying you into the hotel wearing next to nothing."

"Pardon? Next to nothing?" She asked sleepily. She shook her head and stared at him through half-closed eyes and he watched as realization dawned.

"Oh, God! Where are my clothes?" She scrambled to sit up fully as she looked around the rear of the car.

He still had his arms around her and refused to let her go until he was sure she was awake enough to stand up.

"Xander, for goodness sake, put me down." She put her arms against his chest and shoved herself away from him. He didn't want to let her go, but he could hear the panic in her voice.

He kept his arms around her, refusing to give in to the pressure she exerted. "Calm down, there's no rush."

She shook her head. "I can't believe I fell asleep like that." She looked dazed and he knew their lovemaking had affected her deeply. He released her from his arms and she all but leapt off his lap. "Don't sit there smiling, help me get dressed!"

He didn't move. He was enjoying the sight of her as she bent over to retrieve her dress from the opposite seat. In her haste to get decent, she seemed to be unaware that she was wriggling her behind in front of his face.

He struggled to contain his grin. She was an absolute delight. His delight.

Chapter Ten

He had brought her back to his own apartment the previous evening, wanting to keep her close, but now Xander wanted to get back to the island as soon as possible. The sooner he got her out of London the better he would feel. Overnight, his security team had alerted him to the fact that Nick had been released from prison a couple of weeks early, and he didn't want her where Nick could get to her.

He left her sleeping while he put his plans into action. He was at the breakfast table when she emerged from the bedroom wrapped in his bathrobe. "You're up early." She sounded surprised and her eyes were still heavy with sleep.

"I want to get on the road as soon as we can." He extended his hand to her. "Come and get some breakfast before we get going."

"You're leaving." She sat down beside him looking stunned.

"We're leaving," he said firmly. "We've a way to go and I want to get there before nightfall."

"I can't go yet!" She looked at him as though he had lost his mind. "I need to go back to my apartment and pack." She jumped up and paced the room, "I've got so much to do." She stopped and stared at him. "How long before I have to join you?"

He looked her over slowly and hoped she wasn't going to protest. "There will be no joining." He fixed her with a steely stare. "I'm taking you with me today." This was not up for discussion. He would make sure she was safe whether she liked it or not.

"Xander," she placed her hands on her hips and tried to stare him down. "I have so much to pack, bills to pay, stuff to put into storage." He said nothing; she would soon realize that he meant what he said. She swung her arms wide, her tone appealing. "I can't do all that in a couple of hours. I need a few days at least."

"Just give me your keys and my staff will sort everything."

"I can't do that," she sounded mutinous and he bit back a curse. He was used to being obeyed, without question. He needed her to obey now when her safety depended upon it. He wanted her out of London and out of Nick's reach as soon as possible. "I've no clothes with me. I can't just sail off to wherever without at least a change of clothing."

"You can and you will." He held her gaze as he stretched out his hand. "Keys. Now," he said firmly.

She surveyed him quietly, nibbling on her lip, indecision evident on her face. "But--"

"No buts, Chloe." Her safety was too important for him to give into her pleading. His gut twisted at the thought of any harm coming to her, but he also realized he needed to convince her that it was in her best interests to accompany him. "Nick has been released early and we're leaving town this morning."

Her face lost all color and she dropped into the chair across from him. He watched as she clasped her hands tightly around the chair seat as if needing something to help her stay upright. Small tremors overtook her body. His news had hit her hard and he felt like a first-class bastard. He should have broken the news more gently, but she had pushed the wrong buttons, and he had spat it out with considering how she would react. He reached out and took her hands, enfolding them carefully in his grasp. "You've nothing to worry about, but I would feel better if I knew you were nowhere near him."

"You think he'll want to see me. That he'll come after me?" Her voice shook.

"Sweetheart, in all honesty, I don't know." He stroked his fingers across the pulse points on her wrists as he tried to calm her. "Probably not, but I'm not willing to take chances with your safety." He lifted a hand to cup her jaw and she turned into his caress. "Come with me and let my team sort out your packing. We can pick up some clothes to tide you over until your own arrive, it's no big deal." She gave an almost imperceptive nod, which he took as her acquiescence and he felt the tension ease from his shoulders. "Your own belongings will be with us in a day or two. I promise. It won't take them any longer than 48 hours to get everything packed and shipped."

She nodded her head in agreement, but shock and fear still clung to her. He could feel his rage building and his stomach muscles clenched tight as he struggled to maintain a calm façade. If the bastard came anywhere near her, he'd beat the low-life to within an inch of his life.

"Eat some breakfast." He poured her coffee and passed the cream. "It's going to be a long day, so tuck in." He removed the covers from the dishes on the warming plate and watched as she helped herself to eggs, bacon and a few mushrooms. Satisfied that she was going to eat, he excused himself and went into his office to make a couple of phone calls. He had a lot of organizing to do, and very little time in which to do it.

When he returned he was happy to find her enjoying another cup of coffee. There was a bit more color about her and that pleased him. He noticed that the food on her plate was untouched and he was appalled at the bleak look on her face. She was holding herself rigid, as if trying to control her reactions, but still he noticed her hand shook as she placed her coffee cup on the table. Clearly, she was more distressed than she had let on. Shit! He bit back the curse that tore through him. How long he wondered, would it take her to understand that she was safe with him, that he would protect her from Nick?

Regardless whether she trusted him to protect her, she was bound to feel safer once she was no longer in Nick's vicinity. It was time to get this show on the road. Without preamble, he stuck out his hand. "Keys, please."

For the first time since he had re-entered the room, she raised her head and looked directly at him. Her brow puckered as she frowned slightly. She looked dazed as if she did not understand what he was asking. He wasn't used to having to repeat himself and he bit back the desire to scold her for her lack of reaction. With a muttered curse, he realized she was still in shock. He walked toward her slowly and lowered his tone. "Chloe, sweetheart, I will need your apartment keys so I can send someone over to pack up your things." She reminded him of a timid deer and he made an effort to keep his tone calm even though he was raging at the damage Nick had inflicted on her self-esteem.

"They're in my bag." Her voice was barely a whisper.

"Which is where?" He kept his voice low.

She looked toward the bedroom door, and then seemed to gather herself. She straightened as if deliberately making an effort to pull herself together. "I'll go fetch them."

She returned within moments with the keys grasped tightly in one hand. "You will tell them to be careful with my things, especially," she emphasized, "the book cabinet. It's one of the few things I have left of my mom's."

Her voice quavered and his gut twisted with the need to comfort her, but his priority was to get her to the island and away from the city. She didn't look like she wanted to hand over the keys and he was forced to ask for them once again. He wasn't used to having to ask twice for anything, not from his staff and certainly not from a mistress. His teeth hurt from clenching his jaw, as he struggled not to snap out his instructions. He felt tense all over as he struggled to contain his impatience, but he made an effort to appear calm for her benefit. He didn't want to upset her any more than she already was.

He reached out to take the keys from her and she dropped them into his outstretched hand. "Don't worry." He leaned in closer and kissed her softly on the cheek. "My staff are very well trained, they will be very careful, with all your things. I promise."

"I will still need to go back to the hotel. I need to collect a few things there and check out."

"No need," he assured her, surprised by the relief that flowed over her features. "My staff has already taken care of that. I think you will find everything in order." He pointed toward her small suitcase standing by the door. Alongside her suitcase stood the various boxes and packages, which had been delivered to her room the day before. The boxes had been neatly retied and assembled in a stack.

"Find something to put on, but be quick, sweetheart. I want to get moving."

She looked undecided and her gaze skittered toward her suitcase. Her eyes were wide and her face had leached all color. He wanted to take away the haunted look in her eyes and sought to distract her with the promise of a shopping trip. "You have ten minutes to get dressed and then we're going shopping." He looked pointedly at his watch, and then pinned her with his eyes. "Nine minutes, forty-five seconds and counting." Awareness flared in her eyes and he sighed with relief. At last, a reaction. He struggled to contain his grin as she shrieked and headed across the room to her suitcase. She was getting over the shock he had given her. "Don't hurry on my part; I'm not averse to taking you home with no clothes. I quite like the thought of you walking around naked for a day or two."

Chloe giggled. "In your dreams!" Aloud, she scoffed at the idea, but her body pulsed at the thought of being laid bare and available to his demands. She quickly crossed the room to collect her suitcase. "Give me five minutes," she said over her shoulder as she headed to his bedroom to get dressed.

Chloe couldn't believe how rapidly things were changing in her life. She had come to town intending to stay overnight in order to attend an interview yet, here she was, two days later the official, signed, sealed and delivered, mistress of a Greek business tycoon. Her head was still spinning with all that she had experienced. She had needed to relocate in order to escape Nick's wrath however she had never dreamed she would find herself in her present position. By agreeing to become Xander's mistress, she had effectively secured her freedom and safety from Nick, but at what cost?

The pull towards Xander was unexpected, but not, unpleasant. She had never felt attraction so strong on such a short acquaintance. He was like a Greek God and he could easily have posed for any of the ancient statues that graced the world's museums. However, it was more than a physical attraction. For the first time in a long while, she felt safe.

She was still wary of his need to practice sexual domination, but believed him when he told her that he would never force her to do anything she didn't want to. She had no fear that he would strike out and hurt her in a moment of rage, yet she couldn't explain her lack of fear. She had known him barely 72 hours and she knew instinctively that she could trust him.

If she was afraid of anything, it was the thought of disappointing him. She recalled the first time they had made love; he had demanded that she look at him and hold tight to the bedstead. She had felt a little awkward at first, but it had felt incredible to give in to his demands. In a strange way she didn't yet understand, it had been liberating to allow him to take control. Yet, she feared there would be more requests, some that she may not find so easy to fulfill. She wondered what would happen then. Would he be patient with her or would he get tired of waiting for her to meet his needs – needs she didn't even fully understand?

She worried her bottom lip with her teeth, as she struggled into her trousers. The club where he had taken her catered to all kinds of kink and she began to wonder exactly which kink he enjoyed. She bit her lip. He had said they would take things slowly; that he would train her. She didn't want to think about what would happen if she couldn't please him. She shied away from considering what kind of future she would face if he terminated their contract early and cast her aside.

She chided herself for her doubts. She had agreed to be his mistress; she had signed his contract and agreed to his terms. She had to trust him. She had to believe that he knew what he was doing. Xander had promised to make her life easier and she was going to put aside her doubts and grab the chance at happiness.

Determined to look forward and not back, she finished pulling on her clothes and exited the bedroom to find Xander waiting for her.

He smiled as he looked her over. His eyes traveled slowly from her head to her toes and back again before he met her gaze. "Ready to go?"

Her breath caught in her throat at the heat in his eyes, and she felt like he had caressed the length of her body. Not trusting her voice, she could do no more than nod in response.

"Let's move." He placed an arm around her shoulder and guided her out of the apartment door and toward the lift. They entered the lift, and for a moment she studied their reflection in the mirror-lined walls. Like herself, he was casually dressed in jeans and a sweater. He wore designer brands and she wore chain store; he looked sophisticated and glamorous and she felt frumpy and under-dressed even for a shopping trip. Her stomach plummeted. How could she go shopping with him looking like this? She was sure that the women he normally dated were glamorous. They wouldn't have left the house looking like she did now. What was he doing with her? People would think he had lost his mind!

As the lift dropped, he placed an arm around her middle and pulled her back against him. She met his eye in the mirror as he held her close. "You are beautiful." He stared directly at her reflection, his eyes demanding that she believe him, and she wondered how he had known what she had been feeling. She watched as he bent his head and kissed the side of her neck. His hands skimmed up from her waist and caressed her breasts as he murmured in her ear, "You are a beautiful and very desirable woman. Never let anyone tell you otherwise." Even at a whisper, his voice held an authority that made her insides quiver. She closed her eyes, overcome with longing as he nibbled at her throat. She had to get a grip; they were going shopping, not heading to the bedroom.

***

Chloe was in a daze. Going shopping with Xander was like nothing she had ever experienced. Life with money, she surmised, was very different from life without.

A chauffeur driven car had been waiting when they departed the lift. They headed straight over to Knightsbridge and a discreet little boutique where Xander appeared to be well known. Immediately, Chloe felt out of place and out of her depth. It wasn't the kind of shop she would normally visit. She was sure they would have nothing that she could afford.

The sales woman greeted Xander like an old friend, and they exchanged kisses to each cheek in the continental style before embarking on a conversation in rapid French. Chloe's school-girl French was no match and she was unable to understand most of what was said. They obviously knew each other well and Chloe suffered pangs of jealously as she wondered just how well Xander knew the other woman.

As if he had been able to read her thoughts, Xander introduced her to the vendor with a smile on his face. "Chloe, let me introduce you to Madame Lefraye. My sister, Sophia, swears she is a genius at coming up with just the right designs. I have asked her to help you choose some suitable outfits, both for every day on the island and for the events I have coming up in the near future."

"Please, call me Chantelle." Madame Lefraye held out her hand. "There is no need for such formality between friends." Clasping Chloe's hand, she led her away from Xander towards the fitting rooms at the rear. "Xander, take a seat while Chloe and I go and find what she needs."

Chloe was startled at the easy familiarity with which she told him what to do. She cast a backward glance at Xander who stood watching their retreat and smiled when he shrugged his shoulders affably before calling out, "Don't take too long, we have a plane to catch."

Once in the seclusion of the dressing room, Chloe stripped down to her underwear to allow Chantelle to take her measurements. She had to sit and wait while the saleswoman went to fetch a range of items for her to try.

After what felt like forever, but in reality was probably no more than ten minutes, Chantelle returned. Two assistants, who between them wheeled a clothes rail bulging with items for Chloe to try, accompanied her into the dressing room. Chantelle pulled a very smart looking trouser suit in pale grey and a silk lilac blouse from the rail and handed them to Chloe. "Please try these for fit. I thought they would be good for traveling."

The silk of the blouse was soft and caressed her skin while the trousers fit like a dream and hugged the curves of her waist and hip, without so much as a bulge. The short fitted jacket was neat and nipped in to show off her slim waist. Chloe slipped on a pair of socks and donned the high-heeled ankle boots to complete the outfit. She surveyed herself in the full-length mirror and was pleased to see that she once again looked respectable; she no longer felt disheveled. The outfit was demure, but at the same time smart and feminine. She admired the beautifully cut fabric and knew that the outfit would cost a lot more than she would have ever dreamed of spending on a suit.

"Bon!" Chantelle nodded happily, "That is a lovely fit. Do you like it?"

"Who wouldn't?" Chloe replied.

"Right then, we'll put that in the 'to keep' pile," Chantelle said. "If you'll remove that outfit we'll get on with the next."

Chloe quickly stripped off the trouser suit and handed it over to one of Chantelle's assistants. Chantelle handed her a light wool dress in a deep blue and as she fed her arms into the sleeves she watched puzzled as the grey trouser suit, along with several other pairs of trousers in varying colors, were placed on a separate rail. The second assistant was sorting through a selection of blouses and moving them to the other rail.

The wool dress was warm and comfortable and just what would be needed on a cold winter day. It was an everyday dress, and one that she could imagine wearing around the house. It would also be suitable for work with its high neckline, long sleeves, and mid-calf length.

She looked in the mirror and was surprised to see that the fabric clung to her every curve, accentuating her high bust and narrow waist. She looked flushed and sexy, and she bit her lip with indecision. Was this the image she wanted to portray to Xander on a daily basis? For so long she had played down her sexuality, hiding her figure in shapeless clothes more suited to someone far older than herself. Did she dare flaunt herself in something this figure hugging?

The dressing room door opened and Xander strode in. Chloe was startled and jumped when Xander bit out, "What's taking so long?"

She spun around to face him. "Sorry, it's my fault. I'm being a bit slow making my choices."

His eyes traveled over her body, taking in all her curves as he skimmed her length. His tongue flicked across his bottom lip and his nostrils flared. "We'll take it." He didn't so much as glance at Chantelle and her assistants as he issued his order, but kept his gaze firmly fixed on Chloe. "It's a good thing I came to help you then."

"I think we can manage, thank you." Although she strived to be polite, Chloe struggled to keep the note of censure from her voice. His eyebrows rose at her disguised rebuke and he fixed her with his stare. As if sensing the tension between them, the younger assistants giggled. Chloe watched, embarrassed, as Chantelle ushered them around his tall frame and out of the room, pulling the door closed behind her. She had enjoyed trying on the beautiful clothes, clothes that she would never be able to afford to buy and had wanted to take her time in making a selection. However, it appeared that Xander was going to take that decision away from her and she couldn't help but feel disappointed. She wondered if, like Nick, he was going to dictate her wardrobe. Her stomach hollowed out and her enjoyment in the shopping expedition waned as her mood sank.

She closed her eyes and slowly counted to ten. She wanted to regain her composure before she faced him. She reminded herself that they were playing by his rules. If he wanted to choose the clothes his mistress wore, then fine. She wasn't happy about it, but it was what she had agreed to, and therefore she had no right to complain.

Xander leaned back against the door and watched as she struggled to control her reaction. She was clearly not pleased that he had taken the choice away from her. The pulse beating wildly at the side of her throat betrayed her agitation and he held his breath as he awaited her response. She had to learn that he was the Master in their relationship and that he demanded no less than total obedience. It shouldn't matter what the situation. If he chose to instruct her to don or remove a particular item of clothing, he expected instant compliance.

Her eyes opened and he met her gaze head on. "If you'll step outside and let me get changed, I can be ready to leave in a few minutes." Her voice was low and his stomach dipped at the disappointment in her tone. She was clearly upset and trying not to show it and he felt like a bastard. The whole point of the shopping trip had been to cheer her up and take her mind off the threat Nick posed. He could have just taken her measurements and sent a member of staff shopping on his behalf, but he had wanted to give her the pleasure. Now he had robbed her of it.

But step outside? That was not going to happen. He knew she couldn't possibly have chosen everything she would need in the short time he had allowed her, but he had found that having her out of his sight for even a while had been intolerable. Knowing that she was only a few feet away and stripping off, he had needed to seek her out.

"I'd rather stay and watch. Have you chosen everything you will need?" He watched her closely, struggling to read her expression as she veiled her eyes briefly with a downward sweep of her lashes.

She worried her bottom lip before she tilted her head back to look at him. "Not really." She cast her eye over the dress rails. "Chantelle thought the trouser suit would be alright for traveling, and I quite like the dress I'm wearing." She smoothed her hands down her thighs caressing the fabric and molding her shape. "I'm not too sure it's practical for island life or for work though."

To hell with practical. The dress fit like it had been made for her and he intended to enjoy seeing her wear it. "Well, I've already said we'll take it, so that's one decision made."

"But Xander, it's very expensive for a day dress!" She looked askance and he couldn't contain his grin.

"Treat yourself. Hell, treat me." He threw her a wink. "It's very sexy." His cock twitched and his stomach muscles tensed. "The anticipation of removing it and revealing what it covers makes it worth every cent."

She gasped and he knew she had recognized his desire. Her pupils flared in arousal and fed his need. He strode across the room and took her into his arms. He lowered his head and kissed her thoroughly until she was clinging to him for support. When they broke apart, they were both breathing unevenly and he had to keep his arms around her to support her.

"Stop worrying about money, or how much things cost." He stroked down her back until he held the rounded cheeks of her behind in his hands. He pulled her in close and rubbed her against his rigid length. "If you bought out the whole damn shop, my bank manager wouldn't even notice."

He brought a hand up to fist her hair and gently tugged her head back so that he could look directly into her eyes. "I'm going to call Chantelle back and tell her what you need." As she made to voice her objection, he forestalled her. "No buts, Chloe. We need to get moving and time's marching on. Go grab the trouser suit and put it on." He leaned in and kissed her gently before he released her. "As long as Chantelle has all your sizes," he was satisfied with her small nod, "then we will ask her to pick a selection to suit you and our lifestyle." He wanted her to be comfortable with him paying for her clothes, but he was determined that those they did buy would be a lot more flattering than those she already owned.

She had told him about Nick's propensity to dictate the clothes she wore and the fact that he chose styles that were far too old for her and terribly unflattering. He was determined that was a crime she would never accuse him of. He adored her figure and couldn't wait to see her dressed in clothes that would embody the passionate woman that she was trying to hide. Left to her own devices, he was sure she would pick no more than a few basic items to get her through until her own clothes arrived. He had to make sure that she was prepared for every eventuality. He didn't want her to feel embarrassed if a situation arose for which she didn't have the right outfit. He knew women, and there was no way he was going to let the designer- clad partners of his friends make her feel inferior. "I am not trying to dictate what clothes you wear, I just need to ensure that you have enough to get you through until your own arrive." He clasped her shoulders as he focused directly on her face. "I'm sorry you're disappointed, but we do have a plane to catch. You can shop to your heart's content when we're out of London. Scotland isn't the end of the earth, Edinburgh and Glasgow both have great shops, and you will absolutely love the designers on the Continent." He leaned in and kissed her until she was moaning softly at the back of her throat. "Now, be a good girl and get changed as quickly as you can."

As he strolled towards the door to call back the saleswoman, he caught sight of Chloe scurrying behind the clothes rail to remove the dress. Considering he had already seen and tasted every inch of her, he found her modesty refreshing but also a little sad. She was a very attractive woman with a very passionate nature, but she had had all her self-confidence undermined. He would do everything he could to rebuild her confidence in the time they were together. He could hardly wait until she had the confidence to bare all and put him through his paces. He was quietly confident that the day would come and that it wouldn't be too far in the future.

As Chloe changed, he gave Chantelle his instructions and asked that she arrange for everything to be packed and delivered to the airport in time for their flight.

Chapter Eleven

It was good to be back in his workshop. Xander ran his hands over the smooth oak, enjoying the warm tactile feel of the wood. He much preferred to fashion his creations from strong natural materials rather than the more modern chrome and steel. The playrooms at the Marquis Clubs were highly regarded due to his designs, and the quality of the equipment helped to keep them a step ahead of the competition. He enjoyed using his hands to fashion new and innovative equipment. He loved the buzz of creating a highly sensual piece that he knew would give pleasure.

Woodwork was only a hobby, but one he had enjoyed since boyhood when visits to his father's boat-building yard had introduced him to it. He didn't have the time to build every piece himself. He designed, built and tested the prototype and, if the design was successful, he passed it over to a woodworking company that would duplicate his design, making the apparatus available to be distributed exclusively to his clubs. The workshop attached to the Scottish house was his place to relax. He looked around, taking in the racks of wood stacked almost rafter high with hardwoods in various stages of seasoning; the process which allowed the wood to dry out and slowly harden. The smell of the wood, the natural sap, and the scent of oil and wax used to polish the wood to a smooth finish, brought a smile to his face.

He had not spent nearly as much time as he should have working on his latest design. Since arriving back on the island he had spent time with Chloe, getting to know her better and building up the trust between them. He had not taken her into his private playroom yet, and he was conscious that they would only be here for a few more days. However, he didn't want to rush her. He needed to make sure that she trusted him before he allowed himself to think about creating a scene with her. He needed to know that she would obey his orders and accept any punishment he deemed fit. So far, during their lovemaking sessions, she had appeared eager to follow his lead. However, he knew from their talks, that she still balked at the idea of accepting a spanking.

Any form of corporal punishment was a complete anathema to her, which to some extent he understood in the light of her violent past with Nick. But, he still pushed her. He needed to know that she trusted him not to hurt her as Nick had. He wanted the right to spank her, but only she could grant him that. It wasn't necessarily that he wanted to punish her, far from it. He wanted to control her pleasure. He needed to know that she trusted him enough to hand over control. It wasn't about the control per se it was more what the gesture would mean. If she granted him the right to spank her then she would be telling him, without words, that she trusted him and had submitted to his care. His groin tightened painfully at the thought.

Although he had enjoyed having her all to himself for the past month, and he had made love to her at every opportunity, he still needed her to prove to herself and to him that her submission to him was complete. Nevertheless, he wasn't going to rush her.

He had gradually introduced more control during their lovemaking sessions. He had talked openly about his desire for control but had made sure that she understood it could only come about with her consent. He knew she was wary; with her background that was only to be expected. They had progressed from having her hold the bedstead to having her loosely bound with silk scarves. Last night she had agreed to be blindfolded for the first time and he had rewarded her with multiple orgasms. He had loved listening to her scream out her pleasure as she writhed beneath him. Afterward, she had been exhausted and he had snuggled her against his chest as she fell into a deep sleep. He had woken with a morning hard-on and had torn himself away from her side to creep out of the house leaving her asleep in their bed. He hadn't dared to stay. He knew she was exhausted and had gotten very little sleep the previous night, and he was determined that he would let her rest.

Their time alone on the island had been nothing short of idyllic. He had never imagined that anyone could keep him so occupied that he forgot about work, but she did that and more. He felt more relaxed than he had felt in years, and he was in no rush to hurry back to his business.

Unlike women he had met previously, Chloe appeared genuine. He felt like he knew exactly where he stood with her. As her confidence grew she opened up more, and he became aware of how little artifice she possessed. She didn't employ pretense in anything she did. She called it as she saw it, even if she knew he wouldn't like her take on things.

Unlike other women he had known, she was happy to go without makeup. Her well-scrubbed complexion glowed with health and appealed to him far more than he would have thought possible.

He admired her honesty. She didn't pretend she understood his lifestyle, nor did she lie and fake her enjoyment of the limited exposure she'd had so far. She appeared genuinely interested in the power exchange between the Dominant and submissive roles. To his pleasure, she had poked and probed at his psyche as she tried to understand his need for control and the pleasure he thought she would attain by submitting to him. He was a firm believer in knowledge being power and believed that by feeding her thirst for details he was giving her the power to make her own choices.

He loved her enthusiasm for nature. Unlike most women he knew, she didn't run in the opposite direction when he suggested a run along a windswept beach. It was still early spring and they were hardly basking in tropical temperatures on the island. The winds could still be quite harsh and whip around with a bit of a sting, but she had appeared to relish the fresh air and exercise as much as he did and he had loved the rosy glow the cold nip had brought to her cheeks. Her eyes were bright and no longer bore the dark circles she had worn when he had first met her.

She had thrown herself into the role of Girl Friday with enthusiasm. Her determination to earn her keep had been no mere ploy to convince him of her lack of avarice. She had attacked his post and emails like a woman possessed. She had dealt with queries briskly and efficiently, without fanfare and without looking for praise. She had dusted, polished and generally brought the house to life with her feminine touch. She had, in her own words, 'pottered around' in the afternoons while he had been working over in his workshop.

He rubbed his hand slowly across his stomach. He liked her pottering but was grateful that he worked out every day. Chloe had turned out to be an absolute genius in the kitchen and he was amazed that she had never had any formal training. His mouth watered at the thought of the homemade breads and cakes she had whisked up in the past month. She had taken seemingly innocuous ingredients from his pantry and produced some of the most fantastic meals he had ever eaten, and he had eaten in many of the world's famous restaurants.

She was almost too good to be true. His sister would love her when he got around to introducing them. The thought pulled him up short. What was he thinking of? He knew better than to introduce a mistress to Sophia. He'd been brought up in an old-fashioned household. His father had ruled the roost and his mother had been quite happy to stay home and raise the family.

A lot of continental husbands had mistresses, but they were not the kind of women one took home. Traditionally a mistress was employed to satisfy urges that a man wouldn't impose upon his wife; they were considered no more than paid whores. The idea might be a bit old fashioned in the current day and age, but many in his homeland still subscribed to the idea. He thought of the offer and the contract he had asked Chloe to sign and his stomach sank with guilt. He certainly didn't think of her as a paid whore, but he wondered how others would view her.

He had offered her protection from Nick, but how was he going to protect her from gossip? His temper spiked; he would destroy anyone who even thought about hurting her. He was coming to care for her more as each day passed and would not tolerate anyone showing her disrespect.

His gut clenched as he admitted to himself that he was showing her disrespect. He had offered her the role of mistress and nothing else, determined to protect his pride at the expense of hers. He had even justified his stance by persuading himself that he had made the offer in an attempt to protect her from Nick. She had been vulnerable. Physically and mentally, she had been weaker than she was now, and he had used that to his advantage. He surmised that she would have accepted the post as his Girl Friday or agreed to accompany him as his girlfriend.

He'd still been rattled by the outcome of his relationship with Marie and he'd needed the control, and the safeguarding of his privacy, that the contract had offered. He'd needed to be able to control his relationship with her. She'd gotten under his skin in a way he hadn't expected and he'd been determined to protect his heart. Making her his mistress had allowed him to tell himself it was no more than a business proposition.

He'd hoped to persuade her about the merits of submission, but if not, he'd figured he could always tear up the contract. He'd been a fool.

The bond between them was growing stronger every day and he knew he had done her an injustice. He made up his mind to talk to her about the roles they had assumed. Perhaps if he released her from the mistress contract he could persuade her to stay with him, but he was still confused about the role he wanted her to play. If he tore up the contract which effectively made her his mistress, then what role would she fulfill in his life? He didn't want to employ her, he wanted to fuck her. He could call her his girlfriend, but that wasn't going to be enough.

He didn't like the idea of her not being tied to him in some way. The idea that she could walk away from him at any time she chose drove him to grind his teeth. He had started to want it all; a future and a family. He needed some way to bind her to him. Where before he had panicked at the thought that he may have impregnated her with his seed, now he was praying for just that outcome. However, he knew how he was made, and a relationship based on vanilla sex just wouldn't work for him.

He wasn't looking for Master/slave 24/7 type submission from her, but he did need her submission in the bedroom. He wanted her to submit to his care. So far, she had played along as he had introduced her slowly to bondage and blindfolds. She had submitted to his control in bed but had steadfastly refused to allow him to spank her. Her refusal had started to niggle like a thorn in his side. It meant more to him than simply a negative response. Her rebuff was symbolic of her lack of trust in him.

Until he had her acceptance, he knew he would not have her full trust. If she couldn't submit, he would have to let her go, but the very thought sent his stomach into knots.

He was conscious that he would need to head back to Greece soon. As much as he was tempted to stay on and continue to enjoy the privacy of the island, he had a business to run. He could only leave things in the hands of managers for a limited time before the markets would start to question his disappearance. He needed to show his face.

He could only hope that the paparazzi now had someone else in their sights and would leave him alone to get on with his life. He worried about how Chloe would react once the news media got hold of their relationship, and he wondered how they would portray her. His jaw clenched as various scenarios flickered through his mind, and he struggled to come up with a plan to mitigate the damage.

The paparazzi could be cruel when thwarted and he didn't want their ire to turn toward Chloe. She had suffered enough already, at the hands of the local press, over Nick's court case, and he didn't think she would be able to cope with the international coverage her affair with him would bring. He knew from past experience that the media spotlight would attract all sorts of cranks, but her biggest worry would be Nick. How was he going to assure her that Nick was no longer a threat? He had the means and the power to ensure that Nick never bothered her again and had already taken the steps to ensure her safety. He made up his mind to contact his lawyers before he left the island. He would do whatever he could to mitigate the damage before it hit.

He picked up his tools and set to work. He wanted to finish the chair before they left the island. He hummed along to the tunes playing on the radio as he sanded and polished, completely lost to the task. Time had no meaning as the polished oak took on a beautiful sheen and he slowly caressed every inch of wood and every joint. He had to make sure there were no sharp edges or splinters that could catch a user unaware. The equipment not only had to look good, it had to be safe to use.

He stood back to survey the finished chair. He was pleased with it overall. It looked like any ordinary garden relaxer. The polished wood and the carefully crafted joints concealed the additional positions the chair could assume. Skillful woodwork had incorporated anchoring points for restraints, and levers disguised as decoration could be utilized to reposition the chair's occupant. He closed his eyes as he imagined Chloe reclining on the chair and under his command. His groin tightened as he fantasized about her total capitulation as he teased her to completion.

"What are you doing?"

He had been so wrapped up in his fantasy that he had not heard her enter the workshop. He jumped and felt a little guilty.

"Um… I'm just checking over my finished design. Thinking about all its uses and where it can be placed." He tried to sound brisk and businesslike.

"Well, it looks like a garden chair to me." She walked around him to stand at his side as she surveyed the chair. "Stick it in the garden or on the deck." She smiled softly. "Where else would you put it?"

"Chloe, it's not any old garden chair." He reached out to brush a strand of hair back from her face. "It's a piece of equipment for the club."

She turned and looked the chair over carefully, before returning her eyes to his face. "You're kidding!" Her eyes widened slightly as he slowly shook his head.

"No. It's no joke." He indicated the chair with an outstretched hand. "It is definitely a specialist piece. It would be a waste parked in the garden."

Chloe shook her head in disbelief. Even though he had explained his hobby, and shown her some of the pieces he had designed, she still had a hard time getting her head around the fact that Xander, a highly intelligent and successful entrepreneur, spent his spare time building furniture for the kink community.

"I still can't believe that you spend your spare time building such contraptions!" She couldn't keep the shrillness from her voice.

He looked offended and she watched as he slowly straightened his frame and stood taller. His voice was cold when he asked, "Contraption? Do you not think it's a work of art?"

Her stomach muscles clenched as she heard the bite of disappointment in his tone. She had offended him. For the first time since she had arrived on the island, she became aware of how isolated they were and how alone. If he turned violent, she would have no escape.

Something in his tone set her muscles on alert. She didn't know how to answer him and she felt sick with fear. He was so much bigger than Nick; taller and broader with muscles she had enjoyed but which now looked frighteningly strong. She took a step back, deliberately out of his reach, as she looked the chair over.

She forced herself to relax. He had given her no reason to believe he would turn violent.

"I... I don't think I'd call it art." Her heart was racing as she looked again at the chair. "Yes, I think it's a great garden chair. Yes, I'm impressed you can take some lengths of wood and produce something functional." She took a deep breath as she turned to meet his eye, "I still don't see it as a piece of art."

"But, then you're not looking at it through the eyes of a club user." His tone was softer and he was watching her closely. He looked disappointed and she felt guilty. It was clear that he saw it as more than just a chair. "Look at it again." He gave a lopsided smile of encouragement. "Imagine the possibilities."

"Xander, it looks like any normal garden chair." No matter how hard she looked, she could spot no differences between it and any other garden chair. It was slightly more decorative than the run-of-the-mill she would buy at the garden center, and the materials used were probably a lot more expensive, it was finely sanded, but it was still only a chair.

"Come here, let me demonstrate." His voice was still low, coaxing. She thought she detected a hint of excitement in his voice, but when she plucked up the courage to meet his gaze, his face gave nothing away.

He stretched his hand toward her but didn't move any closer. She held back, still unsure of his mood. "Demonstrate how?"

"If you sit in the chair I can show you the different positions." His smile was encouraging. "I need to check it over anyway and make sure it all works."

"That's it?" She queried. "You want me to sit in the chair while you test the mechanism?"

"Exactly." He extended his palm and she placed her hand within his, allowing him to pull her closer. She closed her eyes and inhaled his scent when he bent and kissed her lightly on the side of her cheek. "Good girl." His whispered praise sent shivers down her spine.

"Right, let's test this baby." His excitement was undeniable and she didn't understand his enthusiasm. It was a mere chair. Nevertheless, if it made him happy she was happy to play along.

"Okay." She approached the chair that was already in a semi-reclined position, "Do you want me upright or reclined?"

He moved to the chair and pulled a lever under the arm. The chair smoothly adjusted and the back came upright as the leg rest tucked itself seamlessly away. Clever. She was impressed when she realized the amount of work he had put into the design to get it to do that.

"Sit down and tell me how it feels."

She sat down carefully on the bare wood. It felt warm and solid beneath her weight and she wriggled herself further back onto the seating area. It felt higher than a normal garden chair, but the seat molded and cupped her buttocks comfortably. She placed her forearms on the armrests, checking the position for comfort. She could quite easily imagine sunning herself on the terrace. "It feels great, really comfortable, in fact."

"Good." He smiled slowly. "How does it feel against your back? Are you fully supported?"

She rubbed her back against the wood surprised to find there were no sharp edges. She rolled her shoulders, enjoying the ergonomic feel of the design. "Yes, it's fine."

"Right, let's put your legs up." Once again, he adjusted a lever and the leg-rest slowly rose, bringing her legs up in front of her though she remained in an upright position. "Was that smooth enough?"

"Perfect."

"And how about this?" The back and headrest reclined and she was on her back looking up at him.

"Even better." She could hear the smile in her voice as she told him, "All I want now is some sun and a good book and I'm happy to stay here."

"A book?" He chuckled. "I think not! You haven't seen the best parts yet."

"What more can there be to a chair?" Even as she racked her brain, she couldn't come up with any other positions for the chair.

"Close your eyes." His voice dropped deeper and she recognized the tone. Her Dom was back and her senses went on alert. "Keep them closed, unless I tell you to open them."

She closed her eyes. From the games they had played previously, she knew that deprivation of her sight would only enhance her other senses, and she wondered what he had in mind.

She felt his breath close to her ear and could imagine him crouched by the side of the chair. "I want you to keep your eyes closed and listen carefully to my instructions." He pulled her hair, tilting her face toward him. "If you follow my instructions you will be rewarded." His mouth came down on hers in a hard, yet too brief kiss. His voice slightly hoarse, he continued, "But, I will punish you this time if you fail to follow my orders. Probation time is over, sweetheart."

Her heart rate increased with his words and she was tempted to call a halt. He had given her a safeword to use at the beginning of their relationship, but she had never had to use it. To date, he had been extremely patient with her and had taken time to explain exactly what he was, or was not, going to do. Today was the first time he had taken her by surprise. For the first time, she didn't know what he had planned, and she trembled in anticipation. She bit her lip as she wondered what would happen next.

"Trust me." His tone brooked no argument. He wasn't asking her to trust him, he was ordering her to.

Heart pounding, she exhaled slowly before taking a calming breath. If their relationship was to progress, she had to place her trust in him. "I do," she whispered softly, surprised to realize that it was true. She had thought she would never trust another man after Nick's betrayal, but she did trust Xander.

"I want you to keep hold on the armrests no matter what." His tone was firm. "And, you must also keep your heels down on the footrests. If you're ready, we'll begin."

Not waiting for her answer, he started to talk quietly close to her head. "I want you to imagine that we are alone in a secluded garden. No one can see us. No one can hear us."

She kept her eyes closed and let the hypnotic tone of his voice wash over her. "Now imagine that you are completely bare and waiting for me to join you."

She gasped at his words, but it wasn't hard to imagine the scene he had set. She could feel moisture pooling between her thighs.

"I don't have the necessary equipment at hand; as, believe it or not, this wasn't a scene I planned." He sounded slightly pissed off. "So for now, you'll have to use your imagination." He whispered in her ear. "Your hands and feet are bound to the chair rests. When the chair moves, you move with it."

Before she had time to wonder in what way the chair was going to move, she heard the turn of a dial and could hear the faint rumble of a cog in operation. Her legs started to part and she gasped in anticipation. "Keep your heels down!" Xander's retort was sharp as she started to lift a leg. Quickly lowering her foot back onto the rest, she held her breath as she waited for the outward motion to stop.

When she thought she could spread her legs no further, the movement stopped. She had felt her skirt ride up and expose her panties as the chair opened. She blushed as she imagined him surveying the proof of her arousal. She knew that there was no way he would have missed the damp spot.

"I love seeing proof of how much you want me." His breathing was slightly ragged and he sounded like he was standing in front of her, but she didn't dare open her eyes to check. Suddenly his hand cupped her mound and her eyes flew open. She looked directly up into his taut features. He was standing between her splayed legs.

"Close your eyes. Now!"

She quickly complied, but could not get the look of him out of her head. His eyes had blazed with lust and she knew that he wanted her. Her insides started to pulse and her stomach muscles tightened. What was he waiting for?

She arched her back slightly, thrusting out her chest. She tilted her pelvis and ground herself against his hand.

"Behave." He gave a small slap between her legs that caused her to tense as she felt the sting on her swollen bud.

She gasped in pain, and then sighed as the heated sting unexpectedly turned to pleasure. She was rewarded by the sound of his soft groan. She was glad to know that she wasn't the only one feeling aroused. Once again, he cupped her, grinding his palm against her sensitive folds, but not enough to give her the release she wanted. Her inner muscles clenched and pulsed with need and she was unable to keep still.

"Xander, please--"

"Silence!" His sharp retort cut across her plea. "You are to say nothing. I want you to concentrate on how you feel. Nothing else." She felt his fingers trail softly across her inner thighs.

"This chair," his fingers continued to draw smaller and smaller circles as he stroked his way towards her core, "is built to facilitate pleasure." He slipped a finger beneath the edge of her panties and stroked into her wet slit until she was unable to contain her moan of appreciation.

"I can position you in any way I desire." She felt his breath against her wet and sensitized flesh as he spoke and she shivered in anticipation. "I can have access to all of you." He thrust a finger deep inside her, but once there did not move. "I can indulge all your fantasies, and create some new ones." Her excitement grew. She needed him now. Her insides quivered and she kept her eyes closed as she tightened her internal muscles around his finger. She rocked herself gently against his hand, seeking the friction she needed.

"Naughty!" Xander chuckled at her efforts as he applied pressure to keep her still. "You get your release when I grant it, and not before."

She wanted to weep with frustration. Surely he was joking? She risked opening her eyes and met his stare head on. His eyebrows rose as if in disbelief that she had dared to defy him and he shook his head as he returned her stare. "That is going to cost you." His tone was icily firm. "Close. Your. Eyes."

Her stomach turned. He really did not look happy with her. She swiftly shut her eyes. She wanted him to get back to what he had been doing before. She had felt so good, and now, she felt guilty because she had disobeyed his command.

"We will discuss your punishment later." His voice was quieter, yet still firm. "Agreed?"

She didn't like the idea of being punished, but she hated the fact that she had disappointed him even more. She thought for a moment about his words. He had said they would 'discuss' her punishment. She could live with that. Surely, she surmised she could veto anything she didn't fancy. She surprised herself when she heard herself murmur, "Yes, sir."

"Louder!" Xander stroked the side of her neck. "Repeat your answer clearly in order that there can be no confusion and no doubt. Are you agreeing to be punished for disobeying my orders?"

"Yes. Sir." Her voice rang out loud and clear, and she heard him release his breath on a deep whoosh. She kept her eyes closed as she wondered what he was feeling and what his next move would be.

Xander took a steadying breath. Hearing her call him sir, naturally and without prompting, had astounded him. His heart rate accelerated as he realized how much she was beginning to mean to him. He wanted her more than he had ever wanted any woman.

He looked forward to the time when he would take her into his playroom. He would only take her there when he was convinced that she really wanted to be with him. When he was sure that she was committed to Xander the man, and not Xander the tycoon. He needed to know he could trust her, and more importantly, that she was his.

He saw her submission as a sign of commitment. The fact that she had been abused in the past and had argued against any form of punishment scene only made his desire to spank her stronger. He needed to spank her. He needed to know that she was not afraid of him and that she trusted him not to hurt her. He wanted to introduce her to the thrill of an erotic spanking; wanted to see her bloom under the caress of his hand, not shrink from him in fear. He craved the control only she could grant him and cursed the fact that he had not had longer to plan this scene with her. He would have liked to have their first true scene somewhere a bit more comfortable than his open workshop. He was determined however that she would not step inside his playroom until she had agreed to be put across his spanking stool.

His concentration had been so complete that it took a moment or two for him to realize that a helicopter was circling overhead. He wasn't expecting visitors and cursed whoever was about to interrupt his time with Chloe.

It looked like she had heard the rotor blades also. He watched as she tilted her head back and to the side as if trying to discern the direction the noise was coming from. He was elated that she didn't open her eyes or comment, even though she was clearly puzzled.

"Look at me." He leaned forward and grabbed her hands, helping her into a sitting position. He tugged the hem of her skirt down, covering her damp panties. "Take yourself back to the house until I find out who it is." He pulled her up into his arms, kissed her briefly on the lips and then turned and patted her on the behind. "Scoot!"

Chapter Twelve

His visitor was none other than his contracts manager, Yanis, who had urgently required Xander's signature on a land deal he was negotiating. While she had wished the man away, Xander at least, had seemed pleased to see him. Both of them were sequestered in the study, reading and discussing the documents Yanis had brought with him.

Chloe sat at the large kitchen table preparing vegetables for their evening meal. It was apparent that Yanis would be staying the night as the helicopter had left several hours ago and had not returned before darkness descended. She had seen a very different Xander in action today.

She looked around the large, farmhouse-style kitchen, attempting to memorize all its features. He hadn't said, but she had the feeling that they would be leaving the island very soon and she didn't know if she would ever return. She had enjoyed her time alone with Xander and felt selfish because she did not want to leave the island. She didn't want to have to share him with anyone else. The dynamics of their relationship would change when they were with other people, and she feared the change.

She wondered how he would present her to the world when they left the isolation behind. Would she be his dirty little secret? A mistress, hidden out of view, and visited only when he required sexual release. Or would she be expected to stand by his side, publicly declaring her commitment to him?

She now knew the real reason Xander had removed himself from public life and she feared the reaction of the paparazzi when he reappeared with her at his side. Would they scrutinize her background and bring her assault into the limelight, shaming her for being a victim and holding her up to ridicule? Or, more likely, make snide remarks about the lifestyle they shared, discussing what they might do together, on the late night TV and comedy shows. Her stomach churned and she felt slightly nauseous.

Alone with him, she felt safe. She felt secure. No one could hurt her. Would he stand by her side when the press cast aspersions on her character? Would they call her a coward because she hadn't left Nick earlier, or, in the light of her relationship with Xander, would they call her worse and speculate on her apparent desire for men who inflicted pain. She had not yet experienced the pain of punishment but, having had several talks with Xander on the merits of his lifestyle, she had come to understand that there were different types of pain and that some could be erotic. She had been surprised at how turned on she had become when he had pinched that little bit harder than normal on her nipples or, earlier in the garden chair, when he had swatted her clit. The graze of his teeth across her skin caused goosebumps to rise and when he had nibbled her flesh and nipped with his teeth her excitement had spiked. There was no doubt her attitude toward pain had changed since she had met him.

She thought back to earlier in the day, and what had nearly transpired in his workshop. Her inner muscles pulsed as she recalled the way he had made her feel. Would she have felt even more had she been truly bound to the chair, she wondered. Would she ever get the chance to find out? She closed her eyes as desire washed over her and she replayed this morning's scene in her head. He had sworn to punish her for disobeying his command, and yet, upon arrival of his employee had apparently forgotten his promise. She felt aggrieved and cheated out of something she could only imagine. She wanted to keep him to his promise. She needed to be alone with him, and she cursed Yanis under her breath.

She had been so lost in her thoughts that she had not heard Xander enter the kitchen, and she jumped when his hands came down atop her shoulders.

"Easy." He gently kneaded the tense muscles around the base of her neck. "Relax." He continued to manipulate her flesh as he continued, "I came to tell you that Yanis will be staying for dinner."

"I kind of figured as much, so I am well into my prep." She indicated the vegetables before her on the table. "I am assuming he will also be staying the night, so I prepared a guest room for him." She tilted back her head, resting it against his stomach as she looked up into his eyes. "Is that okay?"

"Yes. Thank you." He leaned forward and kissed her upturned mouth softly. "It is regrettable that we have company tonight. I wanted to talk to you before we returned to the mainland." He kept his eyes fixed on her face. "There are a few things we need to discuss before we leave." His accent sounded more pronounced and she assumed that whatever he wanted to discuss was causing him some disquiet.

"That sounds ominous." Her stomach churned as she returned his gaze.

"There's nothing to worry about." He gave her his lopsided smile though his eyes looked grave. "We'll talk later when we are alone. For now, however, I need to return to Yanis in the study. What time will dinner be ready?"

She sighed softly. It was obvious he wasn't going to enlighten her until he was ready. "Give me another hour. Do you want to eat in here or in the dining room?"

"Here will be fine, as long as you don't mind us sitting in the kitchen." The smile he now gave her was wider, and more open. "I love watching you concoct your delicious offerings and the smell coming from the oven is heaven."

"Flattery will get you everywhere!"

"That's what I'm hoping." He waggled his eyebrows comically, but his tone was serious and belied the frivolity of his remark.

His mood had her puzzled and worried. What had changed since this morning? They hadn't had more than a few moments alone since Yanis arrived, yet she sensed the change in him. She had caught him looking at her several times and his expression had been thoughtful, as if he was trying to figure out what to do with her. Perhaps, she pondered, familiarity bred contempt and he had decided that he no longer wanted her as his mistress.

She knew she had disappointed him with her level of submission. There were things he wanted that she felt unable to deliver. She had been frightened of allowing him to spank her; the thought of pain did not turn her on and she didn't understand this need in him. However, since the episode in the garden chair when she had discovered the flare of heat his swat to her clit had aroused, her curiosity was piqued. She wanted to experience the so-called pleasure/pain that he had described to her. He had promised to punish her, and she wanted the spanking he owed her. He wanted full control sexually and, although she enjoyed the extra dimension he had added to their lovemaking, she still found it hard to deny her body and let him take control of her responses, but she was willing to learn. She would do whatever he wished, if he would only allow her to stay with him. Her problem with submission had been more an issue of learning to trust, than the act of submitting her will. She had thought he would give her more time to get to know him better, to learn to submit.

She wanted to weep. He needed total control and she had been unable, so far, to grant him his desire. Her stomach sank as she contemplated the future without him.

She wondered if he was intending to pay her off and send her away. Would leaving the island signal her departure from his life? She felt almost numb with imagined grief.

She knew he found her desirable. Until the arrival of the other man, he had been unable to keep his hands off her and had made love to her at every opportunity. She thought back over the day and realized that today was the first time she had woken alone. They had not made love once during the daylight hours. Her spirits sank and then rallied as she remembered their interrupted interlude. Xander would have made love to her if the arrival of Yanis hadn't distracted them both. Thinking about how she had felt prior to his arrival, Chloe realized she wanted more. She needed Xander to finish what he had started that morning, and, she wanted his promised punishment. She would not allow him to deprive them both of the completion they needed.

Surprised and determined by her decision, she busied herself finalizing the meal as she set about concocting her plan. She wasn't going to make it easy for him to give her up.

***

The meal was a relaxed and informal affair. Xander had opened a bottle of Shiraz to go along with the tender beef she had served with early new potatoes and vegetables. The conversation had flowed easily between her and the two men, and she had basked in their praise of her cooking.

The raspberry Pavlova she had produced to finish off the meal had brought forth groans that had sounded positively indecent, and she couldn't tear her gaze away from Xander as he closed his eyes in apparent bliss when his mouth closed around a spoonful of the creamy confection. She would have sworn she heard him moan. The same kind of moan he gave when he was aroused. Her sex started to throb and she was taken by surprise when he opened his eyes and looked directly at her. "Save some of this for later." He gave her a slow wink and she felt herself flush.

Looking flustered, Yanis stood up and moved away from the table. "I'll erm… I'll just head back to the study to finish off."

"I'll join you in a moment." Xander didn't turn to look at the other man, who fled the kitchen with indecent haste.

"We've embarrassed him!" Chloe was mortified.

"He'll live." Xander's tone was cool. "I've got another hour or so of work to complete with Yanis and then I'm all yours." He looked at the remains of the creamy meringue on its platter and smiled. "Keep that somewhere cool. I'll be back for more."

"I'm glad you liked it," she said, pleased that he appreciated her efforts. She started to clear the table.

"Oh, I do." Something in his tone made her stop and look at him more closely. The heat in his eyes flared as he leaned toward her and whispered, "It will taste even better when I am eating it off your body." He turned and sauntered out of the kitchen, ignoring her outraged gasp.

She had completely cleaned the kitchen and still Xander had not returned from his study. She felt restless and on edge as she wondered how much longer she would have to wait. Apprehension with regard to the chat he wanted to have left her unable to settle, and she wandered around the house, straightening cushions, and rearranging flowers which didn't need rearranging.

It was getting quite late and she was starting to feel tired. She decided to take herself off to bed, sure that Xander would join her later when he was free. She ascended the stairs and made her way towards the master bedroom. Her eyes were drawn towards the door at the end of the corridor. It was the door to his playroom. The room she had not been allowed to enter so far. In the pit of her stomach, she knew they would be leaving the island soon and she wondered if he ever intended to take her inside.

She checked furtively behind her, almost as if she expected to see him standing there awaiting her decision. She wanted to see what lay beyond that door. She needed to see what the room contained. Would it be better or worse than she had imagined? Surely, a little peep couldn't cause any harm? She talked herself into advancing toward the door. Hand outstretched, she grasped the handle and swiftly turned it before her courage deserted her.

To her surprise, the door swung open and she swiftly stepped across the threshold before she turned and closed the door behind her. She reached out against the wall and threw the switch, which would illuminate his private room. She stood with her back against the door as she took in everything she could see.

It was a large room decorated far more plainly than she had imagined. The high ceiling and walls were painted a stark white. The floor was bare with polished boards and the occasional rug. On a raised dais, in the middle of the room, sat a huge four-poster bed. However, unlike period beds she had seen in the past, this one wore no romantic drapes. The posts and rails of the bed were clearly studded with different types of anchor points. There appeared to be some kind of leather sling suspended above the bed that made her shudder. It looked more like an instrument of torture than a means of giving pleasure.

She advanced slowly into the room and looked at the equipment lined up against the walls. In the center of one wall stood a large St Andrew's Cross, a piece of equipment she recognized from her visit to the club. Hung on the wall to the side were a variety of paddles, canes, floggers, and whips, and she wondered which was Xander's preferred tool.

Against another wall sat a piece of equipment which looked remarkably similar to a vaulting horse you would find in a gym. It had a well-padded top but, apart from that, the only apparent difference she could see was that this one had a variety of handholds and hooks attached around its base. It didn't look that frightening.

She turned and spotted the spanking stool, a little out of the way and toward the corner, it was sat next to what looked like a Victorian nursing chair. Her skin warmed as she imagined being spanked by Xander and her nipples swelled with arousal. The friction of her swollen nipples against the lace of her bra caused her excitement to soar. She thought back to Xander's promise of punishment and her insides started to weep. She had been on edge and sexually needy all day. He had left her high and dry this morning and her libido now needed feeding. How much longer was he going to be before he stopped work in his study? Did he not realize that she needed him now!

She looked longingly at the spanking stool. She had never imagined that the thought of being spanked would arouse her, and in truth, she wasn't sure if the reality would feel anything like she envisaged. Did she dare ask him to spank her?

She deserved to be able to try out his lifestyle before he decided that it didn't suit her, she thought mutinously. He owed her at least one spanking.

A large illuminated cabinet took up an alcove and she wandered across the room to view the contents. Her breath caught in her throat as she surveyed the many sex toys displayed within on glass shelves. The obvious ones such as vibrators, dildos, and love balls, she instantly recognized, but there were many that were completely new to her. She tilted her head to one side as she surveyed what appeared to be a rope of various sized plastic beads. A curved metallic hook with a ball at one end also caught her attention, but she couldn't figure out its use. She wondered whether Xander actually used all of the items in his cabinet or if they were just for show.

"Which do you fancy trying first?"

Startled, she spun and lifted her head to meet his gaze reflected in the glass. His eyes devoured her and she tingled under his gaze. His stillness was slightly unnerving and her mouth felt dry. She licked her lips, rendered speechless by his sudden appearance. She hadn't expected to confront him in his playroom and was embarrassed to be caught prying into his private space. As he approached, she turned to face him. He had removed his shirt though he still wore the dark pants he had donned earlier for dinner. He was also barefoot, which explained why she had not heard his footsteps. His sex appeal was undeniable. Her body hummed in anticipation of his touch as moisture pooled in readiness for his possession.

He approached her slowly and she felt like she was being stalked. In her mind, she likened him to a panther; sleek and strong with the ability to be deadly. He raised his brow and smiled, like a cat who had gotten the cream, when she nibbled her lip in consternation. "Xander, I'm sorry." She rushed on a little breathlessly, "I just couldn't resist a look around before we left the island." She cast her gaze down afraid to see the condemnation in his eyes.

"Don't worry about it. I had every intention of bringing you in here tonight anyway." He sounded very matter of fact, whereas she felt startled.

"You did?" She raised her head to look at him. "Why?"

"Because it was time." He had stopped a short distance in front of her. He reached out a hand and trailed his fingertips along the line of her jaw before he stroked lower over her throat and beyond to the curve of her breasts. "Because we are through playing games." The tone of his voice dropped deeper. "You agreed to be punished for this morning's infringement, and here," he indicated the room with a sweep of his arm, "is the best place to carry that out."

"Oh." She exhaled a shaky breath as she wondered just what she had agreed to. An image of Nick striking out in temper flashed across her mind and had her stepping back from him.

"What do you intend doing to me?" She couldn't help that her voice shook. She felt confused. On the one hand, the thought of being spanked scared her witless, on the other, the thought of being completely at his mercy left her quivering with need. If he wanted to spank her, then so be it. She had definitely earned her punishment and she wasn't about to let him renege especially if it was the only way she had of holding onto him. The thought of a future without him in her life appalled her, and she was determined and desperate enough to push her doubts to the back of her mind.

Xander removed his fingers from her abdomen and stepped back a little. "I'm not sure…" He tilted his head to one side as he surveyed her closely. "I think that you need to learn more control." He kept his tone even and measured as he watched for her reaction.

"This morning," she reminded him sharply, "you said we would discuss my punishment."

Good. He liked that she hadn't forgotten his words. It showed that she had been paying attention to what he said and not just enjoying the sensations her body was experiencing.

"Correct." He gave her his broadest smile of approval. "That's exactly what I did say." He extended his hand toward her. "Come. We will get comfortable for our discussion."

She placed her hand in his and he grasped it as he led her toward the Victorian chair where he intended to sit with her in his lap.

"Is there any point in getting comfortable?" She stopped walking and eyed the spanking stool warily. "You may as well just go ahead and get it over with."

He admired her pluck. The way she was looking at the stool as if she would like to condemn it to the woodpile immediately made him want to laugh aloud. She obviously had the idea in her head that he intended to spank her, and by the look on her face, didn't relish the prospect.

Simply spanking her would be too easy. His cock twitched at the thought of her bent over the stool with her arse in the air, and he reconsidered his rebuttal of the idea. Perhaps, it would be interesting to see how far she was willing to submit to his punishment.

"You're right." His tone cool, he dropped her hand and stepped back. "Strip. You have thirty seconds to get yourself naked."

He sank onto the padded chair and crossed one ankle across his knee as he watched her follow his instructions. He couldn't get his head around how quickly she had complied with his order. There had been no argument, no gasp of offended pride, just a quiet dignity as she had set about divesting herself of her clothes.

He had planned to have a serious talk with her this evening with regard to their relationship, and how they would go forward from now on. He had berated himself on and off all day for forcing her into becoming his mistress. If she was going to stay with him, if she was going to submit to him, then he needed it to be of her own free will and not because he had put pressure on her, or because it was the only way she felt safe. He never wanted her to feel fear again. Not of anyone else and certainly not of him.

She had allowed her clothes to pool around her feet and now stood before him bare. His fingers itched to touch her and he clenched the sides of the chair in order to control his impulses. She met his stare with a defiant glare but betrayed her nervousness when she swiped her tongue across her dry lips. His girl was doing so well. He felt so proud of her. She had come a long way in the short time they had been together. He wondered how much further he could take her, and if tonight would be the night she finally relinquished control.

He pointed to the floor between himself and the spanking stool. "On your knees."

She folded herself gracefully into position and he clenched his teeth as he struggled to contain his impulse to haul her onto his lap and impale her on his erection. His cock surged, the blood pounding through him in strong steady beats, as he surveyed her down-bent head. He needed to maintain control; he had to think of something other than enveloping himself inside her. His mind scrabbled to come up with anything other than her, and then he remembered her curiosity at the cabinet.

"You were looking in the cabinet." He reached out and wrapped her hair around his hand. He pulled her head back and looked into her eyes.

"Which of my toys did you like best?" His voice was no louder than a harsh whisper and he mentally berated himself for letting her get to him.

"I didn't really choose a favorite." Her words were stilted and low.

"But something in the cabinet interested you." He watched as her shoulders tensed. "What was it?"

"I wouldn't say it interested me." She lifted her head and looked warily at him. "I just wasn't sure what it was."

"Describe it to me."

She briefly described the shape and color of the object that had drawn her attention, and he smiled inwardly.

"Do you know which toy I mean?"

"I do." He smiled broadly, as he relished the prospect of introducing her to the toy. "I think you'll enjoy it."

"But what is it for?"

"I think perhaps it is better that I show you." She tensed and looked slightly apprehensive, but did not object.

"Now, however, it is time for your punishment." He indicated the sloping stool in front of her. "Climb aboard."

When she didn't move, he repeated his command. "Now, Chloe! I do not want to have to repeat myself again tonight. Is that clear?"

"Yes, sir." She gingerly moved toward the stool. He snagged an arm around her waist and lifted her onto the stool shaped in an inverted 'v' position. Her top half lay on the cushion-padded slope and she had to stretch out her arms to reach the handholds at the bottom of the slope to help her maintain her balance. Her legs relaxed against the opposite slope as her behind rested on the well-padded apex. He bent and swiftly cuffed her ankles to the sides of the stool and awaited her objections. When none were forthcoming, he walked around and manacled her wrists to the front of the frame.

He ran his fingers around and under the restraints. "Comfortable?"

"Yes, sir." She sounded excited and he struggled to contain his moan of arousal.

He adjusted a lever and the stool position altered slightly. It didn't move far, but it was enough to stretch her legs and have her standing on the tips of her toes. The position would allow her little advantage against him. She would have no choice but to submit to his mastery of her body.

She gave a small whimper and he stroked her back gently. "It's alright.

There's nothing to be frightened of." He continued to caress down her back and across her buttocks in a very non-sexual way as he waited for her to calm down. "Do you remember your safeword?"

"Yes, sir." His heart lurched at her continued use of the phrase and he wondered if she was truly coming to accept him as her Master.

"Good girl."

He had to remind himself that she was new to all of this and to slow things down. He crouched at the front of the stool and lifted her head in order that he could look into her eyes. "The lesson I was aiming to teach this morning was about control. As your Dom, it is my right to grant or deny your pleasure." Her eyes widened as if he had shocked her, but she didn't say a word. "When I tell you to close your eyes, I don't expect to see you gazing at me. When I demand silence, I don't want to hear a word. When I ask you not to move, I expect you to keep still. In here, you call me Master. Do you understand?"

"Yes. But--"

"No buts, Chloe. Those are the rules of this game." His tone was harsher than he had ever used with her before, but he wanted to make sure that she understood his intent. "What I demand, you give. Unless, of course," he quantified his statement, "you decide to safe word."

He held his breath as he awaited her response. When she said nothing he released his hold and stood up moving out of her line of vision.

He continued to talk to her as he wandered over to his cabinet to withdraw several of his favorite toys. "We're going to have a little session where you will practice self-control." He ran the anal beads, that had so fascinated her, through his fingers. "I am going to teach you some new pleasures, sweetheart. You can move as much as the stool allows. You can scream as loud as you want, this room is soundproof." He had returned to her side in time to hear her gasp aloud and he bent and whispered in her ear, "The one thing you are not allowed to do is cum."

She turned her head and looked him straight in the eye. "That's cruel!"

"Wrong, sweetheart." He leaned forward and kissed her softly. "It's control. Its pleasure beyond what you can currently imagine. It's an exquisite form of torture."

He stood up and walked around to her rear. He stripped until he was as naked as her then bent to retrieve his toys, which he placed on a nearby table. The sight of her rounded arse cheeks caused a bead of moisture to form on the tip of his cock and he bit his lip as he fought for control. He craved the day when he could bury himself in her forbidden entrance.

He ran his hands over the rounded globes, parting her cheeks with his thumbs as he ran them down the crease of her ass. She tensed and he watched as her puckered entrance tightened as the tips of his thumbs skimmed its surface. His fingers dipped lower and he found her already wet and swollen for him. He loved her response.

He knelt between her legs and slowly kissed and nipped his way up the length of her inner thighs. As he reached the apex, she tried to close her legs; an impossible task with his shoulders wedged between her thighs. His tongue lapped up the moisture that seeped from her body and he listened to her moans of pleasure.

He withdrew from between her legs and stood up. He leaned against her, allowing her to feel his erection between the cheeks of her arse as he bent forward and stroked his hands up the side of her body until he was caressing the underside of her breasts. He heard her breath hitch in her throat as she fought to contain her arousal. "Now sweetheart," he whispered against the side of her ear, "we're going to try a couple of my favorite toys."

She stilled and it felt like she held her breath. He massaged her shoulders gently. "There's nothing to be worried about. I promise you are going to feel wonderful."

He straightened and grabbed the silicone vibrator that he had removed from the cabinet. He flicked the switch and the room was filled with the sound of a powerful hum.

"Shit."

He laughed aloud at her expletive. He was going to enjoy this.

Slowly he ran the tip of the vibrator between her legs. He eased it between her folds as he twisted and turned ensuring that it was coated with her juices. He took particular pleasure in pressing the tip against her sensitive clitoris. The little nub was already hard and he knew she would be feeling close to her climax.

"Hold it, sweetheart." He told her firmly. "I will not be pleased if you cum yet."

She groaned aloud at his command. "Soon, though. Please."

"We'll see." He switched the vibrator off before slowly inserting it into her vagina where he felt her internal muscles close around it.

"If you're good, I'll switch it back on." He gave a small slap across her backside to make sure he had her attention. "If you cum before I give you permission, I will switch it on and leave it in position all night." He made sure to keep his tone firm. She would be appalled at his threat, but the idea excited him. One day he was going to give her enforced orgasms until she was screaming at him to stop. He wondered how many she would manage before she was totally exhausted. He stroked himself. Soon, he promised himself. Soon, he would bury himself deep inside her.

He reached for the anal beads and a tube of lube. He poured a large blob of lube into his hand and then wrapped his fist around the beads. He worked the beads in and out through his fist until every inch was liberally coated in the lube. Positioning his feet to the inside of hers, he held her in position as he liberally smeared the remains of the lube into the crack of her arse.

As if she guessed his intention, she fought and tried to wriggle from under his hand. "No. Please. Don't." Her breathing was erratic and she became extremely agitated. He didn't want to distress her, but she had to learn to trust him.

"Shhh.... calm down. Relax little one and I promise you, you will enjoy."

"You're too big!" She cried out.

He smiled to himself, pleased with her opinion of his build. He supposed it was only natural that she would assume he had intended to claim her arse, he had told her once before that the day would come. It wasn't her fault that she didn't understand that first he would have to stretch her so that she would be able to accommodate him. He had the ideal set of graduated butt plugs already in his bag for when that time came. Tonight the biggest thing he was going to insert into her, apart from his finger, would be the anal beads that had caught her attention in his cabinet. Her reaction to those and the strength of the orgasm they produced would give him a good indication of whether or not she would welcome him in the future.

She wasn't listening to him. She continued to wriggle against her bonds as she sought to evade him. She had to learn to trust him to know what would or would not bring her pleasure. She was getting herself worked up and in a state over something that wasn't going to happen and he knew just how to redirect her thoughts. "Calm. Down." He smacked her hard across her butt to get her attention. She immediately froze, and gave a howl of indignation at the slap, but he noticed that she didn't cringe away from him. If anything, he would have sworn she managed to lift her butt higher as if she was looking for another slap. He looked down at his handprint across her right cheek; he covered it with his hand and rubbed the heat into her flesh. "I have no intention of penetrating your ass tonight, so stop."

She gave a moan deep at the back of her throat and he had the impression that she had forgotten all about him playing at her back door.

He hadn't, however.

"Chloe, do you remember the beads you saw earlier?"

"Err, yup." She sounded distracted.

"How does this feel?" He ran the tip of the beads through her swollen slit, before trailing them across her peritoneum and up between the cheeks of her arse.

"Okay, I suppose." She sounded apprehensive.

"Relax. Enjoy." With one hand, he held her cheeks apart as he circled her puckered hole with his thumb. He worked the lube around her entrance and forced his thumb inside her past the tight ring of muscle. She moaned loudly, but it didn't sound like fear. He suspected his trainee was beginning to enjoy the feelings he was invoking. He partially withdrew his thumb but held her open just enough so that he was able to slip the tapered end of the beads into her. Once the first bead was past her ring of muscle, he withdrew his thumb completely leaving his hand free to roam over her buttocks. He skimmed between her legs and stroked between her folds. He flicked the switch on the vibrator and set it off on a gentle hum deep inside her body. He watched as she started to undulate and her hips bucked gently as she aimed for her release. He bent and rimmed her puckered ring with his tongue as he forced a second and larger bead past her tight muscle. He twisted the end he still held and felt the vibrations that trembled through her body. It appeared she wasn't as anal retentive as he might have expected considering her lack of experience.

Her legs started to twitch and he knew she was close to her release. He switched off the vibrator and held her down firmly as he reminded her that he was in control. "Remember, sweetheart, you are not allowed to cum until I say so."

"Oh, shit. Xander, please. I need to cum now." She bucked against his hold.

"Master, darling." He slapped her backside, "You are to call me Master."

"Yes, Master." He watched fascinated as she once again strained to lift her behind higher as if she wanted him to smack her. He would investigate this phenomenon later, but for now, he couldn't afford to get distracted. He was supposed to be teaching her about self-control, and yet he was struggling to control his own wayward thoughts.

"We get these inserted properly," he twirled the beads inside her anus, "and then I will permit you to cum. Agreed?"

"Okay, but hurry." She didn't sound happy with him. "I'm hanging on by a thread here!" Her voice was ragged. Her body was coated in a light film of perspiration and her limbs were wracked with tremors. He understood how much she was fighting to hold back her release, and how much she was trying to please him. His spirits soared.

He looked at the length of beads protruding from her anus. The first two beads had been relatively small and no thicker than his little finger. She had squirmed a little but had not objected when he had fed those into her. The beads that remained became progressively bigger as the length grew. He wondered how many she would be able to take before she called a halt. "When I tell you to, I want you to bear down. I want you to push back against my hand."

He applied a liberal coating of lube to her crack and smeared it along the length of the beads. "Now! Push your backside into my hand." He watched satisfied as she pushed herself against him and he managed to push the next bead past her entrance. She whimpered a little, but to his delight, kept pushing back against him. "Oh, baby. You are going to feel so good."

He gave the beads a twirl and enjoyed the little moan she could not contain. He needed to get a couple more of the beads inside her. He reached between her legs and flicked the vibrator back on, gratified when he felt the moisture on her inner thigh. It appeared his angel was enjoying herself. He set the vibrator on intermittent pulse. He wanted to distract her, not take her over the edge. Her body rocked and she ground her mound against the stool. He stroked her clit softly and whispered against her ear, "Push back again, sweetheart." He twirled the beads letting her feel his intention. "Another couple of beads to come, and then I'm going to take care of you."

She stilled and he heard her breath catch. "Master," she sounded uncertain, "I'm not sure I can take anymore."

"You can darling." He stroked her clit a little bit harder and faster. "Trust me."

He twisted the beads inside her as he pushed forward at the same time. She was tight, but he managed to slip the next bead past her ring.

"Well done, sweetheart." He leaned across her back and kissed the side of her throat. "Your ass looks amazing. I'm loving the view." The following bead was quite a bit fatter and he would have to work at getting it past her pinched muscle.

He slipped his erection between her legs, rubbing himself against her vulva teasingly. He could hardly wait to be buried inside her and discover for himself how full she felt with the beads inserted. He straightened slowly, stroking his fingers down her back as he returned his attention to her behind. He turned up the intensity on the vibrator and she moaned aloud.

"Oh, God." She bucked her hips wildly as she tried to force herself back against him.

He grasped her hip tightly with one hand, and on her next move toward him, he pushed hard against her sphincter with the final bead.

"Shit! That hurts." She held herself rigid for a second or two and tried to clench her butt cheeks against this latest intrusion.

"Relax. We're nearly there."

"I can't!" Her voice came out in a wail.

"Yes, you can. Take a deep breath and relax." He molded her cheeks in his hands, kneading the flesh firmly. "If it's really hurting more than you can bear, I'll stop. But, I think you can do this. I want you to do this." He leaned forward and kissed along her spine, pleased when he felt her start to relax.

"On my count, I want you to pant. Concentrate on your breathing and let me do the rest. Okay?"

"Yes, Master." She didn't sound sure, but he would see how things went. If she appeared to be in too much pain he would stop.

"One. Two. Three. Four." She panted in time to his count and he concentrated on getting the final bead past her clenched muscle, he twisted and pushed at the same time, until finally it slipped in and was swallowed by her body. He was elated. She had taken more than he could have hoped.

With the beads in position, he could now concentrate solely on her pleasure. He reached between her folds and withdrew the vibrator. Now he was going to give her the reward she deserved. She had obeyed his every command and he wanted to give her an orgasm that would shake her to her core, and bind her to him forever.

Her thighs were soaked with her own juices and he dropped to his knees behind her. He caressed slowly from her ankles, kissing behind her knees, and up her inner thigh as he made his way slowly towards his goal. By the time he reached the apex of her thighs, she was shaking. When his tongue slipped between her folds to lap up her juices her legs jerked convulsively.

"Master, please." She was near tears and shaking with the effort to withhold her release. "I need to cum. I can't," she sobbed, "hold on much longer."

He rose up behind her. "Soon, darling." With one powerful lunge, he buried himself in her body, up to his balls. "Soon." He twisted the anal beads and felt them rub against his cock through the thin walls of her passage. He started to thrust in and out of her, slow and gentle at first as he rocked himself against the beads. Her internal muscles started to quiver and he could feel her tighten and release around his shaft. She wasn't far off her release. Moreover, neither was he. "Hold it, sweetheart. Just a few minutes more. I want us to cum together."

He increased his efforts and his thrusts became faster and more powerful. His glans started to tingle and blood surged into his cock. He had never felt as hard. His balls had never felt so tight. He was bathed in her wet warmth, and her internal muscles rippled along his length as his excitement grew. He groaned low in his throat as his cock jumped and he struggled to hold off his release. He slowly stroked the anal beads in and out of her back passage, and his own breath hitched as he felt them run along his length buried inside her. "Now, darling. You can cum now!" Her muscles convulsed around him and she screamed out her pleasure as she bucked beneath him. He gripped her hips tightly in his hands and gave a last powerful surge as his cum erupted with a force that took his breath away.

His breathing was ragged, but his body had long stopped the spasms of ejaculation. He continued to play the beads in and out of her body, drawing her orgasm out. He watched in awe as she lifted her backside in the air and rocked against the beads. The moans of pleasure she emitted at each thrust filled him with joy, and when she tumbled into one small orgasm over another, he realized how much she had enjoyed the anal play. It felt like her orgasms would last forever. He was still buried deep within her and had felt each ripple of her delight.

He wrapped his arms around her and held her close. They still needed to talk about their contract. He wanted her to stay with him because she wanted to be with him, not because she was fearful for her future. He held her tightly. How was he supposed to let her go if she decided that she no longer wanted to be with him? It would have been far easier if he didn't have to remember her perfect submission.

She had given him more than he could have hoped for so early in their relationship. She had obeyed every command. Despite her trepidation she had tried new toys and had allowed him to guide her to completion. But the biggest gift she had given, though she probably hadn't even realized it, was her tacit permission to spank her. She had, by her actions, shown that she trusted him.

The sight of her draped across his spanking stool, her backside exposed and vulnerable, had squeezed at his heart. He thought back to when he had first joined her in the playroom. He had mentioned punishment, but he definitely hadn't mentioned spanking. No, that had definitely been her idea. To be fair, he realized, maybe she didn't realize there were other forms of punishment available within his lifestyle. Would it have crossed her mind that enforced or denied orgasms could be a form of punishment? He doubted it!

He wanted time with her to explore all avenues of pleasure and pain. He wanted to see her body wracked with pleasure that only he could deliver. She was his now and he didn't ever want to let her go.

***

Chloe awoke alone the following morning. She didn't remember how she had made it to their bed the previous night, but she did remember the scene that had taken place in his playroom. She had never felt anything so intense. She had never felt so close to another person.

The trouble was, she didn't know whether he felt the same. She had the feeling that he was about to end their relationship and she didn't think she could face that. She wanted to bury her head under the covers and pretend it wasn't going to happen but, unfortunately, her body had other ideas. She felt sick.

She vaulted from the bed and made a swift dash to the bathroom, only just making the bowl in time. She didn't know what had brought on her bout of sickness, but it was something she could have done without. She brushed her teeth and rinsed her face. When she lowered the towel, it was to see Xander standing in the bathroom doorway watching her.

"Are you okay?" He sounded concerned.

"I'm fine. Probably something I ate." She shrugged off his concern. It was more than likely caused by the stress she had been under, but she didn't want to tell him that.

"Maybe." He looked her over. "Maybe not." He murmured cryptically.

She brushed past him as she made her way into the bedroom. Whatever. She didn't feel well enough to play his games this morning.

"Chloe, we need to talk."

Oh, shit. Please, not now. No. She didn't feel strong enough. She wasn't up to this.

She kept her back to him and took a deep breath. She closed her eyes.

She had to toughen up. What had happened to the resolve she had felt yesterday, when she had vowed she would fight for him? She could be whatever he wanted her to be; if only he would let her stay with him.

Maybe if they could put off his little talk until she felt stronger, she would be able to think more clearly. She would be able to make him see sense.

"Xander, please." She wasn't above pleading. "You can see I am unwell, so let's leave this conversation until a little later." Nevertheless, he wasn't to be put off.

"I can't put it off any longer, Chloe." He put his arm around her and guided her gently back to the bed. "Get back into bed for a while. You'll probably feel better if you lie down for a while."

How in hell did he know what was going to make her feel better? She felt her anger start to rise and bit back her angry retort. It looked like there was going to be no way to put him off his chosen course.

She allowed him to help her back into bed. He propped the pillows up behind her and tucked the covers under her arms and around her before he sat on the bed and took her hand. He kept playing with her fingers, stroking the back of her hand. However, he said nothing. His silence was giving her the creeps.

"Xander, whatever it is you want to say, spit it out." She glared at him mutinously. How dare he drag this out and make it worse.

He cleared his throat and finally looked directly at her. "I'm sorry, Chloe."

Oh shit, here it came. The brush-off. The 'it's been nice knowing you, but this just isn't working for me,' speech. She wanted to put her hands over her ears and block out his words. She pulled her hand out of his reach and tucked it under her arm. She couldn't stay strong when he was touching her like that.

"I'm sorry that I asked you to sign that damned contract. I'm sorry I gave you no other choice than to agree to become my mistress." His eyes looked sad, and it took a moment or two for his words to sink in. "Will you forgive me?"

She felt disorientated. Confused. What exactly was he saying?

"Forgive you for what?" She whispered.

"For not treating you with the respect you deserve amongst other things." He leaned forward bracing himself on the bed with an arm either side of her body. "I want to be able to introduce you to my family. I want to honor you, not bring shame upon you."

She wasn't feeling well. She let her head fall back against the pillows as she closed her eyes and tried to wish away the dizziness which had assailed her. His words didn't make sense.

"Xander, you'll have to forgive me." She shrugged and tipped her head to one side as she observed him. "I don't know whether it's because I'm still feeling slightly sick or maybe I'm more tired than usual, but I don't know what the hell you are going on about." He immediately reached up and put a hand against her forehead as if checking her temperature.

"I am attempting to apologize for my past misdemeanors. I have treated you with a lack of respect, and for that, I am most sorry. I humbly ask your forgiveness."

Was he for real? When she giggled, he looked so offended; she had to struggle to contain her laughter. Relief washed over her. He wasn't ending their relationship. What he was doing she hadn't quite figured out, but she would, once her head cleared.

"I bare my soul and propose to you--and you laugh?"

"Propose?" She cast her mind back over his words. She hadn't heard him propose. When had he proposed?

He sighed. "Shall I call a doctor? You've gone very pale." He made to rise off the bed, but she reached out and grabbed hold of his shirt.

"No! Stay where you are until my head clears." Her head was spinning.

She must be sick, but she would have sworn that he had just told her he had proposed. She held tight to his shirt and closed her eyes. "Don't leave me."

"Never, agape mou." He said, using the Greek term of endearment.

She risked peeking at him through half-shut lashes. "Did you just say you had proposed or did I mishear you?"

He placed a hand under her chin and lifted her face up to his. When he was close enough that she could feel his breath across her lips, he spoke softly as he stared straight into her eyes. "You didn't mishear me." He kissed her once. "I want to make you my wife."

Chloe burst into tears. She felt overwhelmed and thoroughly confused as she tried to work out why she was crying. She wasn't normally the weepy type, so why had his proposal prompted a bout of tears? She was happy. More than happy.

"Did I say something wrong?" He backed away from her with a look of absolute dismay on his face.

"Nothing!" Shit, he was going to think she was an idiot. "I'm happy."

His eyes widened and he moved towards her. When he spoke, his voice was cool and controlled. "Then why are you crying?"

"I don't know." She struggled to get herself under control and her voice was stronger when she continued, "I suspect I'm just a bit over emotional as I'm feeling under the weather this morning."

She was fascinated by his eyes. He was regarding her with his steady gaze and she would have sworn that he didn't blink when he asked, "Can I take your happiness to mean that your answer is yes?"

"Yes! Yes! Yes!" She threw herself into his arms.

She was happier than she would have thought possible. His arms surrounded her and she felt safe. He had asked for her trust and, ultimately, control of her body and her happiness. She had willingly given him that power. It had felt completely different from the way Nick had wrestled that control from her and then used it to hurt her. She trembled in his arms and he held her closer. She knew without doubt that this was where she wanted to be. Enfolded in his arms. Under his control. Under his care.

Xander lay down beside her on the bed and gathered her closer. "How are you feeling now?"

The thought crossed his mind that she could be feeling the effects of sub-drop after the scene they had experienced last night. He would keep a close eye on her the next day or two and make sure she came through it okay.

She tipped back her head to meet his gaze. "A bit better. Not as queasy."

"Perhaps I should fetch you some ginger ale and crackers," he murmured. "They seemed to do the trick for Sophie when she was carrying."

She went completely still. "You think I may be pregnant?"

He would swear she was holding her breath as she awaited his answer. "The possibility had crossed my mind." He watched her closely to see whether or not the idea upset her and was relieved to see a look of pure joy flit across her face, before she turned and asked, "You wouldn't mind if I was?"

He couldn't contain his smile. "No, agape mou, I wouldn't mind at all," he assured her before he bent to claim her mouth.

The End

About the author

Glenda was born and brought up in the beautiful city of Edinburgh in Scotland.
From an early age she was an avid reader. She became engrossed in reading romance novels in her early teens and promised herself that one day she would sit down and write her own. That dream was achieved with the publication of her first novel, Playing for Keeps.

Also by Glenda Horsfall

Playing for Keeps

Matt is worried! Their relationship is in trouble. Cassie has been begging him to add role-play to their lovemaking, but the kind of role Cassie wants him to play leaves him cold. When he discovers her stash of erotic romance novels, he comes to suspect that what she really wants is dominance.

Matt takes Cassie away for the weekend to celebrate her birthday. She is disappointed that the 'highlight' of the weekend is to be a costume party. A costume party is not the kind of role-play she's fantasized about. She is surprised when she realizes it will be a party for two and that Matt has actually taken her to a BDSM club.

Cassie agrees to be his 'love slave' for the weekend and promises to obey all her 'Master's' commands. Matt is surprised at her enthusiasm and is turned on by her ready acceptance of his domination.

At last, he understands her desire to role-play and Matt indulges her fantasies, along with a few of his own. However, the weekend away has changed their relationship and has taken them in a direction he hadn't foreseen. Now he's wondering if they can survive the changes.

Coming soon from Glenda Horsfall

Playing with Fire

Latest titles from Black Velvet Seductions

The White Spider of Savignac by V. L. Smith
The Love She Wants by Mila Winters
Her Cowboy's Way by Starla Kaye

www.ingramcontent.com/pod-product-compliance
Lightning Source LLC
Chambersburg PA
CBHW030331020726
47493CB00004B/1239